THE LAST NETWORK

By Chris Furlong

This is a work of fiction. Names, characters, places, products, and events are the products of the author's imagination or are used fictitiously. Any resemblance to actual persons, living or dead is entirely coincidental.

Join my mailing list at www.cfurlong.com

In memory of Jason Kreiger and Min Choi

Acknowledgments:

I'd like to thank Ted Zlatanov, Jason Krieger, Jessica Palladino, Tyler Leshney, Matt Kirkpatrick, my Partners at Ultra Mobile, and my wife Tania Mohammad for their help in developing this from the Peared product idea to its final form in fiction.

CONTENTS

1. The House Cat   9
2. Menonaqua   12
3. The Reverse Job   16
4. An Accomplice   18
5. Demo Man   22
6. Debris Field   26
7. Kendra Calling   28
8. Travel Together   31
9. Checkpoint Whiskey   35
10. Launch Crickets   39
11. Nichols P.I.   41
12. The Push   44
13. God Mode   47
14. The Retrade   52
15. Tech Beat LA   57
16. The Illegitimate Firemen of Instagram   62
17. Matchmakers   64
18. Currents   66
19. Pep Talk   68
20. A Bottom   71
21. Office Party   75
22. Future Time   77
23. A Hypothetical   80
24. Unsolicited   85
25. Clone Club   88
26. Harder, Better   91
27. Without America   95
28. Bullets   98
29. Toehold   101

30. Casings   105
31. The Cross   108
32. Back Offices   111
33. Long Haul   113
34. Trolls R' Us   115
35. Dog and Pony Shows   119
36. Pusher Man   122
37. Afterword   125
38. Omar's Army   129
39. We're Only Science   133
40. Bump in the Night   138
41. Friendo   141
42. Go Time   144
43. Job Description   146
44. Twinning   150
45. Layer Fake   154
46. Confirmation   157
47. Sixty-Eight Guns   159
48. Blow Up   162
49. Double Move   165
50. Mastro's Ocean Club   168
51. Slate   170
52. You Gotta Walk   172
53. Business Class   176
54. Struck Down   180
55. Accelerator   184
56. Ricochet   187
57. One Door Opens   192
58. Another Closes   195
59. Stateless   199
60. Tijuana Dutch   201
61. Pillow Talk   203
62. Tired but True   206
63. Network Control   208
64. Decipher   211
65. Lines   215

66. Home Away   218
67. Sunseeker   222
68. White Bordeaux   224
69. Cabernet Sauvignon   226
70. One Year Later   228

1. THE HOUSE CAT

Rabbit Wilson put his phone down and looked across the conference room table at his lieutenants. They'd been with him through thick and thin. Over the last decade, a lost decade, he'd been to their weddings and he'd been to their funerals. He covered for their frailties and they had given him their best.

Season after season, they harvested bytes of video and ground them into pennies of ad revenue. It wasn't what Rabbit imagined when he moved to California, but it had saved him. Without these people, he'd have stayed lost. He would have never recovered from Frank Meyers. He would have never gotten back up after his divorce.

Now he was going to leave them high and dry.

He hadn't told a soul. He had never shared his special idea. He locked it inside and carried it alone, waiting for this moment. It was a strong idea, it was his best idea. He was sure of it because it had stuck with him all these years. There had been no need to tell others, no need for validation, that would only risk the future. Now the future was here. His first impulse was to get up, walk out of this glass box, and never come back. No words, no goodbyes, just a ghost disappearing down the hall. It would be a power move for sure, but people would forgive him once they knew.

They would call it grief, even though it was joy.

He looked out the office windows to the street below. Traffic was moving freely down La Cienega all the way to Wilshire. He could be home in 40 minutes, packed in an hour, and at LAX in time for the 3 o'clock to Detroit. If he moved quickly, he could beat his brother home. He could have first dibs on their old bedroom. He could unlock the desk drawer and be the first to know if the old man had kept his word. Everything hinged on his word. A part of Rabbit didn't trust it, and he had good reason not to. The old man had been difficult his entire life. Cancer seemed to change that, but you never knew. Death freed people. It made them wildcards.

It was time to leave the office. He would take bereavement and give his two-week notice at the same time. Smash House had been good to him, but it had also been a prison. Rabbit once had a very bright future. A dozen years ago, he was part of the 'Legendary Class' at Square 90 Ventures. That one incubator program produced three IPOs, three exits, two successful companies, and only two failures. The talent they assembled, Ka$ia, Kendra Godfrey, Frank Meyers, Vic Khan, Rabbit Wilson. It was LA's first and only real threat to Silicon Valley. Only Rabbit had fucked up his chance. One brutal blow broke Frank's jaw and made Rabbit a pariah.

The local venture capital community never forgave him. Only Ka$ia had given him a second chance. She hated Frank as much as he had, and he knew why. While he liked to think he did it for her, he hadn't. He did it because Frank was a smug, know-it-all, piece of shit. He did it because the arranged marriage between their startups was doomed from the beginning. While it made sense on paper, no one lived on paper. He tried telling his board that. He tried telling his investors that. No one listened. Failure is what they got.

He spent the next decade running Ka$ia's company. While she redeemed him, she also used him. She used him as her ticket to founder's rewards. He spent day after day on the content farm, while she ran off to speaking gigs and tech conferences. His hard work translated into her equity. Now he was free. He would finally have the chance to bring his special idea to life.

That is if the old man kept his word.

Everything hinged on his word.

"I think you all know that my father, Bear Wilson, was battling cancer. His battle is now over. I need to leave and make arrangements. Lisa, can you take over? While I appreciate everyone's sentiments, I need to be alone right now."

Rabbit stood and quickly left the conference room. He did it before anyone could get up from the table. He didn't want their hugs, he didn't want their condolences. He wasn't going to manufacture sadness. This was his victory and he was going to enjoy it on his terms. The words he uttered greased his exit. Nothing more was needed. He was free, and no one could stop him. He finally had the one thing everyone used to hold him down, money.

In a town that gave out ninth chances, he had only gotten one. Now everyone was going to learn how big a mistake they had made. That is, if the old man had kept his word.

Everything hinged on his word.

2. MENONAQUA

Rabbit pulled off the main road and drove the rental through miles of slow turns and spinning tires. The winter road, formerly hard dirt and frozen crystals, was dissolving into the early spring slop he hated so much. Town was filling up with condos, but out here people were in retreat. Rabbit looked for mailboxes that served as landmarks only to find rusty bent poles. A mile later than expected, he laid eyes on the carved wooden bear that guarded their driveway. He pulled the SUV out of the muck onto gravel. Grip returned, and the last two hundred yards were an easy ride. Nothing had changed here. The shingled cottage with its wraparound porch and neat piles of firewood was identical to the memory he carried of the place.

Growing up, his father had been a man of constant motion. Always on the road, never speaking about his business, completely unapologetic. His mother had been the one to watch him play CYO hoops, to drive him to hockey, to show him how to use deodorant. Only here, at the summer lake cottage, was Bear Wilson a regular dad. Here they went fishing and played catch in the yard. This was the place Rabbit thought of when he thought of home.

There it was, still in mint condition. Rabbit got out of his rental and ran his hands over the hood of the forest green Grand Wagoneer. He walked in a slow circle, tracing his fingers over the wood paneling. Three decades old and not a scratch. He'd be shocked if there was more than 100,000 miles on it. Dad never drove his baby between here and Ann Arbor. That was the regular car's job. This was the vacation car. Its job was to take them to ice cream, to drop people at the lake, to get mom from the club when she played euchre and drank herself senseless.

The engine was warm. His father never parked it outside. Stephen was here. His brother had beat him to the cottage. Rabbit looked up at the kitchen window. The big oaf was hunched over the sink, dirty blonde hair, ruddy complexion, mustache. The older he got the more he looked like the Brawny Man. He was a Great Lakes guy through and through, never comfortable south of Chicago or east of Buffalo. Bear had been like that. Rabbit took after their mother's side. Before Bear, she'd been Jessica Riley. An Irish Catholic from upstate New York. Pat Riley's second cousin, as a matter of fact. Rabbit looked like him. Tall, lean, and hungry with a face dominated by wolfish sunken eyes and a huge white smile. It flipped between two expressions: charismatic seduction and scorned fury.

Stephen must have flown the Cessna in from Hibbing last night. His wife didn't like him flying over the lakes, especially at night in the off season. Rabbit didn't blame her. Stephen had gone down twice, both times in remote country. His brother scavenged the north, acting as a broker for mill byproducts. Flying was a necessity and an occupational hazard. If the old man was true to his word, Stephen could give that up.

Gravel crunched under his hiking boots as Rabbit walked towards the two-story cottage. It was one of the few up here that had been winterized. His father had planned his retreat a long time ago. Rabbit pictured him behind the wheel of his Cadillac driving from one industrial behemoth to another, pitching pension plans and dreaming of the day when his world would be nothing but woods, dunes, and stock picking. He was always going to disappear up north. Now he was gone.

The screen door creaked open and Stephen appeared on the porch with two cups of coffee.

"So?" Rabbit asked.

"So, what?" Stephen passed a cup to Rabbit then took a seat.

"You know. Was it there?"

"That's your first question?" Stephen blew on his coffee, one eye cocked towards Rabbit.

"You flew the Cessna over the lakes to get here. It was the first thing you went for. Have you even seen him yet?"

"No, the funeral parlor opens at ten."

Rabbit hunched down opposite Stephen, his eyes locked on his brother. "Was it there?"

"Yes."

"How much?"

Stephen took a sip, enjoying the ability to torture his brother far more than the coffee itself. "A lot more than I expected to be honest. I mean how much money can one crank with a *Wall Street Journal* subscription and CNBC make?"

"I'd know if you answered me Stevie. Don't make me smack you."

"You remember the last time you tried that? You can end up in the pond again, I don't care if it's frozen."

Coffees were placed on the table. Both men stood, eye to eye, toe to toe. Stephen wrapped his arms around his older brother, squeezing tight and lifting him off the porch. "He did the best he could. I'll miss him."

"I know Stevie, I know. I'll miss him too."

"Rabbit, there's $47.5 million in a Merrill brokerage account." He burst into laughter. "$47.5 million fucking dollars."

"Holy shit. Did you call Jack Thomas?"

Stephen dropped him. "Yes."

"And?"

"He said there have been no changes to the estate. We need

to see him after we go to the funeral home. He'll read the will then."

"That son of a bitch." Rabbit opened the porch door and led them inside. " So, what are you going to do with your half?"

"I'm giving up the life. Getting off the road and being a dad. I'll build that cabin I've always talked about, maybe buy a trophy business in town just to say busy. The rink or the bowling alley, nothing serious. You?"

"I'm going back to LA and I am going to show those fuckers a thing or two."

"Still on that Rabbit? Still sore after all these years?"

"You mean Dad, or my first startup?"

"I mean both. They go hand in hand."

Stephen was right. His father had pushed him west. He had forced him to make his own life, in his own field. Rabbit had tried to learn from his father. He asked him to teach him his business. Not the life of a salesman, but his father's other skill, stock picking. Bear's bosses never let him join the investment side, he was too good a broker, but that's where his heart was. Selling retirement plans was just a means to an end. When Bear had enough money to invest for himself, he quit and disappeared up here. Rabbit showing up, wanting in, wasn't a part of the dream, so Rabbit was pushed away, rejected.

Bear pushed Rabbit so hard he landed in Los Angeles and never came back.

For fifteen years Bear lived alone. He didn't tell his sons how well he was doing, only that it gave him satisfaction. Every Christmas he drove to Hibbing and in the summer Stephen's family visited the lake, but that was it. Nothing else. Just a man who wanted to be alone and the promise that he'd do them right in the end. Now that Rabbit saw what right looked like, he could accept it. His father's dream was about to enable his, and that tilted the scales.

3. THE REVERSE JOB

Rabbit sat in the corner of an office swiping right. They were downtown in one of those older buildings that had been subdivided into suites and filled with fly-by-night professionals. Across from him, a man wearing a virtual reality helmet was gesticulating wildly. He'd been doing that for the last two hours. Pointing into the air, jabbering away in Hebrew, sometimes getting up and pacing. Rabbit watched as the man stood and walked into his waste basket again. Skittles spilled out of the bin and dribbled across the floor. These people were supposed to be the best, but who could tell? Yelp didn't cover this line of work.

The VR helmet was connected to a lab full of guys somewhere in Israel. Tel Aviv maybe? Rabbit wasn't paying close attention. He'd perk up when they told him they could do the job. In the meantime, he had Tinder and time to kill.

His stomach rumbled. He should have eaten lunch before coming; now he was stuck. The man had Rabbit's external hard drive and Rabbit didn't trust him alone with it. Finally, the man removed the helmet.

"We can do it."

"How much?" Rabbit asked.

"Five hundred thousand, maybe seven fifty. We'll need to think it over."

Rabbit looked up from his phone. "How long?"

"Something like this could take six weeks. It could take

more. I need to know what you want the finished product to look like," the man said.

"Swap the graphics with generic icons. Wipe any identifiable marks. I need this to look like fully licensed code. I need papers on it. I'll need a website and a code repo for developers to pull from. Most of all, no one can know it's a knock off. No hint you reverse-engineered a surgical training tool."

The man sat down behind his desk. He looked across at Rabbit. "More work means more time and money. I'll need to put a pencil on it."

"But it can be done?" Rabbit asked.

"Of course, it can. That is not a problem." He answered without looking up from his notebook.

"When you do your quote make sure you have a really sharp pencil. I'm not into wasting time or money. This could be a nice job for you, or it could be a great job for my friends in Minsk."

"I understand. You, my friend, came here on referral, so you also understand what we are capable of. Our work speaks for itself."

"Funny, but I've heard nothing about your work," Rabbit said.

"Exactly," the man replied.

He stood and handed the drive back to Rabbit. They shook hands. Rabbit left in search of burrito.

4. AN ACCOMPLICE

She was sitting in an Adirondack by the fire pit. An open bottle of cab rested against the chair. One sandal was on the grass, the other dangling from her toes. The Pacific sun reflected off the water holding her in a golden embrace.

It had been a long time since Rabbit had seen Kendra Godfrey, and she looked all the better for it.

He peered down from the stone patio and studied her. Something was different about the Ice Queen of AI. He remembered her as a tightly wound metronome, constantly tapping. Sometimes her pencil, other times her heel, but never a still moment. Maybe it was the situation? Their last time together was cooped up in a conference room. Now she reminded him of a calico cat curled around a big glass of red wine.

He waited and watched, sipping his scotch. They were here for a golf tournament. Rabbit played, but usually skipped the corporate events. With the Israeli job still weeks from wrapping up, he had time to kill and wanted to get out of town. Half Moon Bay was a favorite retreat, and he needed the nights to make Platinum Elite.

A mountain of a man walked up from the putting green and gave her a lover's kiss. Malcolm DuBour. He had no idea they were together. Rabbit smiled, so the past and present of outsourcing were an item, very interesting. He'd once gone to dinner with Malcolm in Vegas. It was a tough meal.

Malcolm had five kids, Rabbit none. Malcolm loved yachts,

Rabbit thought boats a waste. Malcolm supported Man City. Rabbit only had eyes for the Lakers. On and on it went, until some emergency or the other pulled Malcolm away. Rabbit had heard rumors about the man; he was supposed to be a fixer of some sort. It was the type of skill one needed to do business in all those remote shit holes. Bags of cash, no-show jobs, favors for favors. Enough about Malcolm; Rabbit wasn't interested in the man in the Nantucket Reds. Kendra, on the other hand, had just what he needed.

He watched as the giant sauntered off, pitching wedge over his shoulder. Rabbit saw his opening and walked down the stairs.

"Kendra Godfrey, as I live and breathe."

"Is that Rabbit Wilson? Wow, it's been awhile."

"The one, the only. You here for the Guardian?" he asked.

"Sure am. You too?"

"Yup. So, you and Malcolm, huh? I shouldn't be surprised, you always had a type." He sat down next to Kendra.

"He keeps me entertained, we'll leave it there. Now Rabbit, I heard you walked out of Smash House just like that. What is going on with you?" she asked.

"I'm on to the next thing and I need some help."

"Now you are speaking my language. Give it to me."

He watched as she dropped her other sandal and perched on the edge of her chair. Her right hand started swirling her glass of wine. Round and round it went until a slow vortex formed in the middle. Nothing had changed with Kendra, she had been in the off mode and now Rabbit had turned her on.

"I'm striking out on my own. Consumer internet, very edgy, self-funded," he said.

"How big?"

"It has the potential to be huge. Truly transformative. I don't want to say too much right now, I'm waiting for my proto to be completed, but I'll give you one word. Teleportation."

"Teleportation?" she asked

"Yes. I call it Peared. None of that sci-fi bullshit. I'm not beaming people up or down. I'm giving people a way to see the world through another's eyes. I'm giving them the ability to do a lot more than that."

"Now I'm intrigued. You need NAM for this?"

"Yes. I need a partner to run the service. Someone who isn't afraid to bring out the old school tactics. I need someone who can press people's buttons," he said.

"You want FriendZone rules?" she asked.

"FriendZone rules," he answered. Kendra took a long slow sip of wine. A smile spread across her face as she sat back down in the chair.

FriendZone Rules was shorthand for the addictive design practices the social network perfected a decade ago. Get people hooked, then reward them with drips of dopamine delivered through never-ending notifications. It was the old way of doing things, when the goal was to keep people on for as long as possible, to make as much as possible through any means possible. After years of scandal and bad press, most companies had moved past that and signed onto the Silicon Valley Code of Conduct. NAM was an exception.

"I've been dying to play that game again, only everyone else has been too scared to. I've got just the guy you need. He's young, but he's got that thing. A real operator. You'll love him. I have dinner plans tonight, then I'm busy after." He smiled and traced her finger down the arm of the Adirondack. "I can do breakfast. Meet me in the morning? I'll have Paolo come down from HQ so you can meet him too."

"Breakfast sounds great."

Rabbit gave her a quick kiss on the cheek and wandered back to the bar. She was hungry for the work. He wasn't surprised. NAM had invented the hybrid AI/offshore model a decade ago. Every aging internet company turned to her to slash payroll and wring the very last dollars out of their fading dinosaurs. Match.com, Cars Direct, Yahoo. All were early clients. Kendra's company took control of each and followed the same playbook. Fire everyone, then have NAM's combination of AIs and cheap foreign labor run the show.

The thing is, Kendra lacked tact. She cut too hard, too deep, and she failed to change tactics when the rest of the industry got a conscience. Instead of reading the tea leaves and playing more ethically, Kendra took FriendZone's dark patterns, addictive tactics, and perfected them. The better the machines got, the fewer people she employed. Now it was nearly all AIs and evil wizards who were master manipulators. Big name clients got scared of associating their brands with NAM's reputation and bookings fell. Now they were on the outs and in need of a marquee client.

Rabbit didn't give a shit about their rep. Kendra had been the smartest person in their incubator program. She could produce like no other. Even better, she'd have to deliver. Her future as NAM's CEO hung in the balance.

5. DEMO MAN

The elevator opened, and Paolo Soto stepped onto the Vampire Floor at NAM. Jason Patric and Kiefer Sutherland stared back at him. Paolo nodded at the mural and bared imaginary fangs, his daily offering to the house gods. From twelve until he left for USC at seventeen, Paolo had been a wannabe Lost Boy. Leather, sunglasses, and shitty attitudes. It was no wonder his parents were thrilled when he left Chile for college. From then on, he was America's problem.

The rest of the building was soulless. Open floor plans, spotless glass and corporate whiteness. The Vampire Floor worked the overnight shift and staffing it was always a challenge. To keep headcount high, standards were dropped, and employees were allowed to take liberties with the space. The lights were always dimmed, most teams worked inside giant tents, and their commissary opened after the main cafeteria shut for the day.

Paolo liked it here. People left him alone. On the lower floors, he'd been bombarded with requests to fix Excel macros and review calculations. Once he discovered the night floor, he moved up there and worked daytime hours in splendid isolation. Kendra didn't mind—he was the guy she put on the hairy problems, the ones people shouldn't know about. Isolation was a good thing.

He hung his backpack on the wall and rubbed his weathered brown hands. A weekend of climbing had left them scraped and calloused. Wandering into the kitchen, he picked up a stale grilled cheese and poured the last of the coffee from the pot. Some would hate this existence, but Paolo quite liked it. The problems were challenging, and Kendra took a special interest in him. Besides, he wasn't going anywhere. Until his green card came through, Paolo and NAM were joined at the hip.

At 10:00, he put his coffee down and put his VR glasses on. It was time to see if Rabbit had something special or if he was just another in a long line of pretenders. The screen went black and everything was silent. He sat back in his leather chair and waited. The void was relaxing, and he found himself drifting off when the system suddenly clicked on. He was on a skateboard accelerating down a steep street. He could hear the wheels picking up speed, crunching small rocks. Wind whipped his face. The view screen shook. He instinctively focused on the road in front of him. There was a blind curve coming up. He could see the ocean on the horizon, a hill on the left, and a steep drop on the right.

He'd never be able to make the turn at this speed. Paolo hadn't skated since high school. It was a miracle he hadn't fallen off by now.

"Hello?" he said.

There was no response, just the oncoming rush of a decision to be made. The board showed no sign of slowing down. He looked down. He was wearing heavy black jeans with knee pads. He had an armored motorcycle vest and elbow pads on. At least I won't get cut to bits, he thought. He looked up—the curve was approaching faster. The skateboard was aimed straight towards the ocean and was picking up speed.

"Hello!" he yelled.

He looked to the left. A giant chain fence was wrapped around the hill to keep rock slides from crushing cars. He turned to the right. There was a small guard rail, three feet of grass and then a drop he'd never survive. He jumped to his feet.

"Stop this now."

Nothing happened. In a panic he shifted his weight to the left. The board obeyed and started cutting back into the on-coming curve. He wouldn't plummet into the sea, but he was going too fast to make the turn. He pressed on his back foot and lifted his front. The board flipped up and the rubber guard of the kick tail dug in, grinding hard into the asphalt, slowing him down. He combined both moves, turning and decelerating at the same time until he was under control.

On the other side of the corner was a scenic pull off. Rabbit was there, leaning against a green Jeep Wagoneer. Paolo steered the board towards him and stopped.

"What did you think?" asked Rabbit.

"I think I'm going to puke," Paolo answered.

"Don't do that; I don't want Eddie to ruin my shoes," Rabbit said.

"Why not, Rabbit? I've got a full stomach, I could ralph up a storm right now. Get some on your pants, too," Eddie said. He was the real-life skateboarder.

"Paolo, this is Eddie, your surro. Your movements in VR controlled him in real life, and neither of you are going to puke. This is a business meeting."

"What the fuck? Why didn't you answer me halfway up the hill? You could have died. Why didn't you start turning earlier?" Paolo asked.

"I was waiting for instructions. Besides, I had another fifteen seconds before I was in trouble."

"Instructions?" Paolo asked.

"Your virtual reality glasses have cameras inside and out. They pick up what you are doing and translate them as commands for Eddie to mimic. His augmented reality glasses place your commands over his eyes. So, he sees symbols that tell him to turn left, turn right, brake. That sort of stuff. I told him not to talk to you, I wanted to see if you figured it out before it was too late. What do you think?" Rabbit asked.

"It's intense," Paolo answered.

Adrenaline pumped through him; his heart raced and sweat ran down his back. He stepped off the board and walked towards the edge of the pullout. The ocean was a couple hundred feet below him. He looked to the left and could see a city in the distance.

"Where am I?" Paolo asked.

"Malibu," Rabbit answered.

"So, everything I do in my office gets mimicked by Eddie?"

"Yes. Now Paolo, can you get people hooked on this?"

"That's not going to be a problem. The problem will be making sure they don't get too addicted."

"I was hoping you'd say that. So, I can tell Kendra that you're in?" Rabbit asked.

"Yes. Get an agreement signed and I'll spin up a team."

"Eddie, give me your glasses and grab the other car. I'm going to take Paolo for a drive."

Rabbit clicked the overlay off and put the AR glasses on. Paolo watched through his eyes as the Jeep started up and turned onto PCH. He tried wrapping his head around what he just experienced. Rabbit had talked a big game over breakfast, but Paolo wasn't prepared for this. Teleportation was only part of what Peared could do. Rabbit had invented a new form of control.

6. DEBRIS FIELD

Rabbit had money, but he still had a reputation. No one wanted to leave their job and join his startup, not even his old lieutenants. It stung, but wasn't surprising. He wasn't the nicest guy, and being an asshole only works when you have leverage. Rabbit was selling a dream, but people thought it just as likely a nightmare. No one wanted to be the next Frank Meyers. Rejected by his colleagues, Rabbit decided to gain leverage with the only chip he had, money. He was going to buy a company and put them to work on Peared.

He spent the summer picking through the wreckage of the LA startup scene. The place was filthy with failure. He found it crammed tight in WeWork sweatshops, hanging on in Westside office spaces, and working out of Valley homes. After a few months, he could lean out the Jeep and catch the scent of rotting ambition on the wind.

He was a man on the hunt.

He had a few rules. First, no venture capitalists. VCs had put him out of business the first time. Control mattered. Whatever company he was buying, he was buying outright. He wasn't trading equity. He wasn't putting together a business plan and there'd be absolutely no power points.

Second, he needed a founder who had the good sense to know he wasn't the alpha. Sure, he'd have to be a leader for his team, but Rabbit needed a person who realized that they had run their company into the ground. VCs were obsessed with geeky dropouts who coded before they had gotten laid. They'd give those shit stains plenty of second chances. Rabbit needed one who understood his genius ended at technology and didn't want to get burnt by business again.

Third, there needed to be a strong team in place. He preferred one that had shipped something before bombing out. Something they could look at with pride and blame the cruel world for not recognizing their work. He wanted a confident group of losers, ones that were ready to get back in the game and just needed a surefire idea to rally behind.

It was a tall order, but he didn't have a lot of options. A company in trouble could overlook a lot of past sins, especially when he was offering cash, upside, and most of all, a real vision. Rabbit was banking on that awestruck look people had after finishing his demo. His prototype opened doors, expanded horizons, blew minds.

In late August he finally found his quarry. Fox had bought a startup called ImmerCast as an experiment in virtual reality broadcasting. They built a streaming delivery network and prepared to do live sports in VR. After virtually no one watched their preseason NFL broadcast, Fox left them to rot on the vine. They'd been in stasis for almost a year and were seriously jaded.

After a week talking with their founder, Sonny Kumar, Rabbit was ready to pull the trigger. ImmerCast had been in the Fox budget to deliver a little over a million in revenue. In that unit, missing budget was a cardinal sin. All Rabbit had to offer was the missing money, and ImmerCast was his. It was a steal. He had a technical leader with serious chops, a tight team that was dying to get back to work, and an easy commute from Hancock Park to their Century City office.

7. KENDRA CALLING

Rabbit stared at a door locked with a keypad. He was trying to get to the parking garage and didn't feel good about this latest obstacle. Somewhere along the way he'd taken a wrong turn. He tried the handle. It was locked, and it was cold. He pressed his ear to the door and heard whirring fans behind it. That was a server room, not a stairwell. Disappointed, he turned and retraced his steps. His phone rang as he walked down the hall.

"Rabbit, it's Kendra. Got a minute?"

"Sure, but first things first. Do you have any idea where my stairs are?"

"My building keeps them in the northwest corner."

"I have no idea where I'm facing. No windows back here." Rabbit reached the end of a hall and paused looking left then right. "What's up?"

"Paolo still can't stop talking about the demo. You need to let me take a ride sometime, maybe I can go out on one of your dates with you."

"Funny Kendra."

"I'm not kidding. I think it would be hot to watch you wine and dine some sexy little strumpet."

"Peared can do so many things, and your first thought is voyeurism. Sorry Kendra, but there are no sexy little strumpets. I'm the child in my relationships. I've been dating divorcees. Women with kids, the type that does barre and only has time for dinner once a week."

"That doesn't sound like you. Still haven't gotten over Diana yet?"

"Oh, I'm well past her. Hard not to be given how things went. No, I'm putting everything I have into Peared. A night out a week is all I can spare. Matches up well with a certain type."

"Well Peared is what I am calling about. We've seen a lot of tech specs—it looks like Immercast has that covered. I like your new COO, Sonny. He has his shit together. What we haven't seen is branding and positioning. Who is the target market? Where are the customer archetypes? What does success look like? We need branding, life cycles, and marketing budgets just as much as the API docs."

"It's coming. I'm meeting with Em Nichols tomorrow. She's leading our product launch."

"You got Em Nichols? Now, that's impressive. I'd love to have been inside your glasses when you pitched her. If Paolo is raving, and Em is onboard, this thing must be good. I'm getting that magical tingle I love so much."

"Kendra, I don't remember you being such a perv."

"The money tingle, Rabbit. You know it's been a little dry around here. I need Peared to make it rain."

"I'm going to drown us all, Kendra. Just give me your best people and stock up on umbrellas."

"That's what I like to hear. Next time Malcolm and I are in town, we are going out for dinner. A double date with one of your cougars. Maybe we'll head out on the boat after?"

"Sounds nice Kendra. Say 'hi' to Malcolm for me."

"Will do. I can't wait to see what Em comes up with."

"Me too."

"And Rabbit, just retrace your steps. It's an office building, the stairs can't be far away."

"You'd think that. I'll see you around Kendra." He hung up and turned left.

8. TRAVEL TOGETHER

Rabbit huddled with Em Nichols in a wooden hut in the back corner of the office. She pulled her fine red hair into a ponytail and rolled up her denim sleeves. "Veni, Vidi, Vici" was tattooed on her wrist. It was as much a warning as an ethos. Every season brought her a new product launch, a bigger challenge, and another notch in her CV. So far, she had crushed them all.

They sat on creaky toadstools while LED lights cycled from pink to blue then back again. A trickling stream projected on the floor, and imaginary songbirds perched in the rafters. The decor was Disney meets cyberpunk. Every few minutes the stream glitched then briefly disappeared. A slightly yeasty smell came from a pile of beer-soaked stuffies in the corner. ImmerCast tradition was that each new hire dunked a stuffed animal in beer, then wrung it into their mouth.

Rabbit's Yosemite Sam was on top of the pile.

This was Immercast's imagination hut. These guys could code, but they had serious limitations as creative beings. Rabbit wanted to tear it down and replace it with a normal conference room. The only thing stopping him was the team's misplaced love for the abomination. They had taken solace under its roof too many times to let it go.

"I didn't realize you were such a big deal," Rabbit said.

"Am I? Who's been talking about me?" Em asked, opening her notebook to a pink tab labeled P for Peared.

"Kendra Godfrey."

"Right, Kendra. The Queen of Machines."

"Not a fan?"

"Let's get started on Peared, shall we?"

Rabbit took the hint and moved it along. Em was Ka$ia's friend. Over the years, she'd done special projects for Smash House. She was Rabbit's favorite creative. Em figured out how her client's mind worked and made sure her pitches were tailored to their thinking. Rabbit for instance, needed to be built from the bottom up. Language and concepts came first. Visuals only at the end after he understood the meaning of everything underneath.

"So, I've been given the demo and spent some time fooling round with the product. I like it. There's a lot we can do here Rabbit. First things first though, we need to invent some terminology," Em said, flicking the notebook pages until she found one filled with crossed out words in neat penmanship.

"Terminology?"

"Yeah, definitions and labels. 'Surros' isn't going to cut it out in the real world."

"Why not?"

"A surrogate is disposable, powerless, and temporary. It's a dehumanizing term that shows a real lack of respect. 'Hey who wants to be a surro today? Head on out in the cold and let some fat ass boss you around.' Does that sound good to you Rabbit?"

"When you put it that way."

"Positioning is everything. Surros are out. Hands and Eyes are in."

"Hands and Eyes?"

"Yup. Hands are the doers. Eyes are the seers. Together they share a Consciousness which makes them a Pair. Learn it, remember it, and believe it with every fiber of your being."

"It sounds good. Hands and Eyes share a Consciousness. Together they form a Pair." Rabbit said.

"Good, I'm glad you like it because it feeds into our new tagline...Travel Together with Peared."

"Travel Together with Peared."

Rabbit paused and looked up into the rafters. Em watched as he began talking to himself, mouthing the words. Hands, Eyes, Pairs. Consciousness. Travel Together. He was stepping into her words like a new pair of shoes. They didn't seem like much, but Rabbit knew—he knew that millions of people would be saying these words, over and over, day after day. They needed to be comfortable, but they needed to be sturdy. He liked the way they sounded. They felt like terms that had always existed, as if Peared lived in an alternate universe and just crossed over.

"Travel Together with Peared," he repeated out loud. "Hands, Eyes, Pairs, Consciousness. Yes, they work well together. I like it, a lot."

"Thank you, but you need to recognize one thing above all Rabbit—Peared is a very dangerous product. It's a control platform. All of our positioning needs to defuse that imbalance. People need to think of each other as equal and willing participants. Otherwise no one is going to want to be a Hand and those that do will be treated like slaves. These terms, this language, it's designed to give Hands permission to drop their guard and let the Eyes control them. If you don't have permission and the perception of equality, this doesn't work."

"Hence Travel Together."

"Exactly. The next step is to dial down the perceived power of Peared. We need to treat it like a toy until people are used to it. FriendZone started as a way to see what your friends did on their weekends, now it's being used to swing elections. If you told people where it would end up, do you think they'd have given it that much information?"

"No."

"Right. There's a whole playbook here Rabbit. Consumer internet is the seduction of soft power disguised as frictionless convenience."

"That's a little above my comprehension Em, but I'll take your word for it. Love the language, the terminology, and the thinking. Any chance you got something I can see?" Rabbit leaned in.

"Not yet. I wanted to make sure you were with me before I went much further. Give me a week or two, I'll have my designers get some looks ready."

"Sounds good. You talk to Ka$ia lately?"

"I checked in with her before taking this job. Needed to make sure there wasn't any issue with us working together."

"And?"

"I'm here, aren't I? You could have handled it better, but she understood. At least that's what she told me." Em closed her notebook and slipped it inside her bag.

"I'll reach out to her when I get a chance."

"You should. We all need friends, Rabbit."

9. CHECKPOINT WHISKEY

"We've passed Checkpoint Whiskey." Sonny Kumar announced.

Rabbit had his back turned to him, ear buds in, head shaking, fists banging on the desk. He'd been cooped up, pacing for the last hour, waiting on the results of the meeting a couple doors down. Now they were in and Rabbit was oblivious.

"Rabbit, we've passed Checkpoint Whiskey."

Still no response. Rabbit began hopping up and down. His slicked back hair fell over his forehead as he rocked out. His fists rattled the desk, shaking things, making items bounce up and down to the driving beat in his ear buds. He was a ball of energy. Sonny heard metal coming out of the buds. He'd never seen this side of Rabbit before. He was always cool and in charge, keeping himself at a distance from the Immercast crowd.

The run up to launch does strange things to people. Sonny for instance, committed completely, rarely leaving the building. He slept in his office, came home on weekends, stopped shaving. He needed complete concentration and no distractions. No detail was too small to fuss over. His wife was used to life as a launch widow. They'd both been through IITs back in India, elite grad programs here, and then on to demanding careers. Pressure was a natural state of being. If he could, Sonny would live in a never-ending build out.

Rabbit, on the other hand, needed to burn his energy. If he hadn't been waiting for Sonny to give him a date, he'd have been at the gym. The busier everyone else got, the less there was for Rabbit. He'd shared all his ideas, answered their questions, and signed off on everything. Now all he could do was wait. He paced, and he rocked out in his office.

Sonny tapped him on the shoulder. Rabbit jumped.

"Whoa!"

"Sorry, Rabbit. I've been behind you for the last minute, yelling for your attention."

"What is it Sonny?"

"We've completed Checkpoint Whiskey."

Rabbit pulled his hair back, removed his ear buds, and slowly wiped his face with a hand towel. The wild man should have never come out at the office. Rabbit made a note to never do that again. He sat behind his desk and motioned his COO to sit.

"You'll have to excuse me. I wasn't able to make it to the gym today. You were saying?"

"The teams had a very open and honest conversation about their statuses. We discussed blockers, workarounds, and timelines. For the most part, we are on schedule."

"Do we have a launch date?"

"I have commitments from everyone for March 7th."

"That's good. Anything I should be worried about?" Rabbit crumpled the small orange towel and tossed it into his gym bag.

"There's some interpersonal issues, but aren't there always? Nothing we can't manage. I'm trying my best to get our guys to play nicer with Paolo and NAM. Like I said, nothing we can't manage."

"What's the issue?"

"Well, some of the access that Paolo is requesting is rather unorthodox. It gives him more power than we'd usually allow to a third party. Some of his requests are frankly beyond reason. Nothing you need to worry about."

"You are accommodating him?"

"In most cases, yes."

"Sonny, were my instructions to accommodate him in most cases?" Rabbit snapped to attention, ready to make a point.

"No."

"What were they?"

"To give him what he wants. Rabbit, I take pride in managing my people and my shop. I don't like to bother you with the inner workings, but it's also important that you and I see eye to eye. When there are conflicts, like there are now, I have a duty to discuss them with you. Rabbit, Paolo is asking for things well outside the Silicon Valley Code of Conduct."

"And?"

"I assumed we are following the code."

"Why did you assume that?" Rabbit furrowed his brow, confused why Sonny was out of the loop on such a central concept.

"Because everybody does nowadays."

"We are not everyone. We are playing by FriendZone rules. Is that a problem for you?"

Rabbit had wrongly assumed that Sonny knew about Friend-Zone rules. Now that it was laid bare, he watched as his COO processed the information and came to terms with Rabbit's true intentions. Death or glory. Nothing in between. He fully expected Sonny to fall in line. His go around with Fox ended with nothing to show for it and after a year spent on the sidelines, Sonny wanted to get back in the game more than anything. Rabbit was offering another bite at the apple; sure there'd be a worm in it, but it was still sweet, especially the option package Rabbit dangled in front of him.

"Not at all," Sonny said.

"Good. NAM's AI has trained on a decade of data. That's fifty client companies, a billion unique users, and over a trillion sessions worth of information. It has seen literally everything ever tried on the internet and can implement those practices into Peared. It keeps our headcount low and reduces risk on our side. Paolo's team eats what they kill. I don't pay them a salary. They take 30% of our ad revenue. The only limits I've given him are to not break local laws. I am backing Paolo all the way. Kendra and I have a history together. I trust her and her company completely. They are going to make Peared a monster."

10. LAUNCH CRICKETS

He remembered this feeling. It brought him back to a time when he whipsawed between panic, rage, and helplessness. It had been a dozen years, but that cocktail was burned deep into his temporal lobe. It was a there as a warning. The last time Rabbit felt this, he'd lost everything.

Don't fuck up again. It told his brain. *Don't shit your pants.* It told his guts. *Punch that mirror out.* It told his fists.

Rabbit paced across the office, hands balled tight. He had to get out of here and pull himself together. He slipped out the back, started for his car, then changed his mind. He needed to walk this episode off. The bright sun and hot air blasted him as he left the office building and started down a dry cedar-chipped jogging trail. A lone black suit lost among the dog walkers and Lycra clad joggers.

The launch had gone flawlessly. What had followed was crickets.

No one was downloading the app. The few who did weren't using it. Rabbit couldn't tell if he had a marketing problem, a product problem, or worse, both. The plan had called for a soft launch. Get Peared into the app stores, make sure everything worked right, and then start marketing once the company felt good about things.

After the launch, there should have been a PR bump. Em had done her homework, reached out to people, and lined up all the usual suspects. Everything looked fine until the night before launch. Around nine, she heard they'd been put on a blacklist by the tech press. Someone was serving up revenge. Maybe Ka$ia had a change of heart about his departure—maybe it was Frank Meyers.

Whoever it was, they had serious pull.

The launch plan called for fifty thousand users from PR. They got two articles which yielded squat. App store optimization was their next free marketing bullet. Only no one searched the App Store or Google Play for teleportation, because it didn't exist yet. The idea was for the news to create a buzz around the first teleportation app. Since that was them, they'd get all those searches.

No articles meant no buzz. No buzz meant no search traffic.

After a week, Rabbit had given up hope that someone would discover Peared organically. It was time to pay for what had not been given. He poured $100,000 into online marketing. It got them a little over twenty thousand installs. A tenth of them opened the app a second time. That was bad. Really bad. Something was wrong with Peared. Either it sucked, or people didn't know how to use it.

They had tried to go general market and missed. Em's colorful commercials had been shelved. The faucet turned off. They needed to diagnose the problem before they went back out there. All Rabbit could do right now was blow off anger. That wasn't especially helpful, but it was a fuck ton better than smashing things.

Or people. He shuddered and told himself that this time was different.

11. NICHOLS P.I.

Em stepped into the Ivy, home of the $8 lemonade and the $25 salad. She hated this place. The shabby chic decor, the garish mismatched pillows, so many roses. If ever a room needed editing, it was the Ivy. The design was best described as grandma on acid which also summed up her lunch date, who had recently taken up micro-dosing.

Betsy Simmons was sitting in the corner at her usual table. She was the Doyenne of Doheny Drive. She was also Em's god-mother. Most of her time was spent reigning over afternoon mahjong, and trafficking in rumor and gossip.

Em walked across the room. Everyone ignored her but Betsy. Her eyes peered out from behind rose-colored glasses, sizing Em up, looking for changes since they last met. Any small clue that could open up an avenue of inquiry. Betsy couldn't help it. She was wired this way and Em knew it. Before coming here, Em evaluated herself as Betsy would, making sure to wear no jewelry, light makeup, and the most minimal on-trend outfit she could find. Look just good enough to not make that the question, but no better, so that the focus would be on the task at hand.

Someone had spiked Em's launch. Three months of hard work flushed down the toilet. She didn't know who and she didn't know why. The first step was establishing a motive. To understand why, she needed to better know who she was working for, and Betsy knew everything about everyone.

She was 72 and had buried three husbands already. She didn't

cultivate information or parse it out judiciously, she was a con-
nector, a switchboard. To sit down with Betsy was to be at the
source of every going on in town. The trick was to make sure
that you had nothing to offer her, otherwise you'd leave having
given up far more than you consumed.

Em knew this too well, which is why she was so careful in her
appearance.

"Dear, you are so severe. You need to live a little," Betsy said.
She stirred her tea and offered Em a seat.

"I live through my work."

"Don't I know it. How come you only call when you need
dirt on people?" She tapped her spoon twice against the cup for
emphasis.

"What can I say? I'm a transactional person."

"We all are, only most of us choose to fake it, so what's this
about?"

"I've been working on a product launch for a tech company,
Peared. Neat product, brand new space, super sexy press angle...teleportation. This should have been a slam dunk. Only the
night before launch, my embargoed exclusive drops out. She
won't tell me anything. I call my back up and tell them it's
theirs. They won't touch it either. Something is fishy, only it's
too late for me to do anything about it. The next morning, I
blast the press release out on the wire and then start making
calls, looking for coverage. One journalist after another turns
me down."

"You got blacklisted."

"Yes, but why?" Em sighed, her eyes to the ceiling, hands
gripping the seat of her chair.

"So, that's why you are here today. Okay, tell me whose company is it?"

"Rabbit Wilson."

"Oh child, not him." Betsy shook her head. "Next time call before you start working for someone. I can save you a lot of trouble."

"Why? It can't be Frank Meyers."

"No, it's not Frank Meyers, and it's not because he's a prick. Even though both of those are true, neither are enough to cause something like this. Nadia Camiso is your reason."

"Who is Nadia Camiso?"

"You mean who was Nadia Camiso." Betsy blew on her tea and raised her eyebrows. She enjoyed delivering the news.

"She's dead? Great."

"Like so many others...Nadia went before her time and very poorly. A lot of people were upset at her passing."

"And she was connected to Rabbit?"

"Yes. It was very complicated, downright ugly, actually. Normally I'd just give you the dirt, but this one is better heard from someone close to her. I'll put you in touch with a friend that was involved. Now, it's my turn. I want to talk about your love life."

12. THE PUSH

Paolo's ass had been torn apart by Rabbit, then by Kendra, and finally by both just to make sure he understood what was at stake. He didn't need those calls, though. He knew exactly what was at stake. Peared was dead in the water and bleeding money. It wasn't his fault that the product was a dud, but it was his responsibility to fix it.

The bitch of it was, when Paolo's team sat down and explained how it worked, users loved it. The challenge was taking that in-person demonstration and turning it into an app-based experience. For the last month they had worked around the clock testing demos, videos, tutorials, and prompts. All their efforts only slightly improved conversion rates. They never came close to how the in-person demonstrations performed.

There was something fundamentally different about Peared. His AI could not find it. His data scientists could not find it. His user experience specialists could not find it. They were following best practices and previously successful patterns. By every known measure of the modern internet, the thing should work.

He sat down with Cristina Gomez, NAM's director of customer feedback. Her appearance was always presentation-ready. You could pick her out of the break room and drop her on Madison Avenue and she wouldn't miss a beat. Today though, she was all tired eyes, chipped polish, and dark roots. She had just completed her third round of customer surveys. The first two had been rather clinical and specific. For her third pass, she decided to go blue sky and see if it was something beyond buttons and interfaces.

"So, what do we have?" Paolo asked, hands running through his hair.

"Awkward."

"What?"

"Embarazoso." She flipped into Spanish to make sure he got it.

"In what way?"

"They describe it a lot of different ways, but it happens right at the beginning. There's this pause, an emptiness. Neither side knows what to do. It just sits there, getting bigger and bigger and then they bail out." She broke eye contact with Paolo, looking past him, out the window, her gaze drifting further and further away as she described the gap.

"When we do the demos..." Paolo thought out loud.

"Ah yes, the demos." Cristina snapped back to the table. "Where we welcome them in, spend five minutes chatting with them over coffee. Where they get to see someone else using the system while we tell them what we are going to do and what they should do. That whole setup time is about getting rid of the awkward." She finished.

"We tested an in-app tutorial with simple tasks to perform."

"And?"

"People did them, but it didn't solve the problem of abandonment. They were another dead end." Paolo hunched over the table, rubbing his forehead, mentally recounting all the ways they had failed.

"That's because afterwards, the awkwardness kicked in. You need to figure out a way to get past that. You need to give them a push." Cristina said.

"A push. Interesting. That's something new we can look at."

"This is a psychology problem Paolo, not a design problem. You have to get them engaged in a common cause before that awkward moment happens. Have them chase Pokemons or something."

Cristina was right. They had been looking at the problem the wrong way. That was the thing about data. If you have enough of it, you think it can solve any problem. It was time to put the machines aside and take a different approach. Paolo realized he needed someone skilled in a different set of dark arts. It was time to call Evan Willis up.

13. GOD MODE

Clip after clip showed the same thing. None lasted more than 30 seconds, but they all felt like an eternity. Paolo had seen many of them before, but they still made him uncomfortable. The pauses, the stilted interactions, the sheer social awkwardness of the whole thing. So much work had gone into Peared, and this is what it had yielded.

This session summed up everything wrong with the product. A man dropped into an apartment building, his eyes fixating on every imperfection in the place. The empty pizza box, the bunched up dirty socks, the horrible lighting that oozed gloomy depression. It made his skin crawl. Paolo looked over at Evan, studying his face hoping that this man had an insight into their problem. They were running out of time and needed to turn things around quickly. Otherwise, this whole operation would fold. Just another one of the million bad ideas that briefly bloomed, then died in the tech hothouse called California.

"See there, that's your first problem. People are just appearing in shitty apartments with no idea what to do. You need to give them a mission. The next problem is that you are not establishing who the boss is right from the start. The Eyes need to lead, the Hands need to follow. You are getting these brutal conversations because the Eyes don't know they have permission to drive. Put me in and watch how it's done," Evan said.

Evan Willis was a polymath who lived in the boundaries between black and gray. Burner, behavioral psychologist, pickup artist, investor. He hacked systems, he hacked people. Paolo didn't like him but could not deny his unique talent. The man could see angles no one else could.

Paolo used him as an asset when he needed to design a solution that was more art than science. Evan carried himself as a pompous techno punk complete with purple hair, Victorian eye glasses, and a black velvet vest. He had a peacock feather pinned to his breast pocket and a white gold chain around his waist. He took his fedora off and put Paolo's virtual reality unit over his head.

They were operating in God Mode, the administrator version built to manage Peared. It was the backdoor into the system and granted them an incredible about of power. In God Mode, you could see any user's location, past history, preferences, friends, and saved clips. It let an admin send commands and messages that weren't available to regular users. It had development modules that weren't ready yet. In short, it was a playground for testing, manipulation, and voyeurism. Evan's eyes lit up when he saw all the tricks available to him.

"I want to pair with that one."

"The woman?" Paolo asked.

"Yes."

Paolo pulled up the profile of a woman in her early twenties. She lived in Santa Monica just off the Promenade. She had never used Peared before, and all Evan had to go on was a profile pic of a tatted-up mod with cherry red lipstick and rockabilly bangs. Paolo connected the two and watched the monitors in front of him. Evan as the Eyes was on the left. Suzy as the Hands was on the right. They were inside her apartment. The interior was a remnant from the seventies. Yellow Formica counter tops and shag carpeting.

"Grab your bag and put some running shoes on. There's no time to lose." Evan directed.

"I wasn't expecting a guy."

"I'm alright. I won't bite. Something tells me you want to be bad. I've got a little mission that's right up your alley. If I go too far, please call me out and I'll back off. Does that work for you Suzy?"

She nodded. Paolo watched, noting how quickly he had gained her confidence. The door opened, then the two were down the stairs and out onto California Ave.

"When was the last time you stole something?" Evan asked.

"High school."

"You ever get caught?"

"Once."

"You miss the rush."

"Now that you mention it..."

"I can see your heart rate picking up. You're blinking faster. The idea excites you. I want you to know that I'm a master thief. I started at age eight and I've never been caught. If you do as I say, see what I see, and follow my instructions, you'll be just fine."

"What are we going after?"

Evan turned his head to the Apple Store across the street. He waited for her eyes to track and center on it, then he pushed the glamour effect from the God Mode which made the door dazzle and for the briefest moment the words 'TAKE ME' flashed over her eyes.

"Everything in there is locked down. I won't be able to."

"The Genius Bar."

They walked into the store. Evan looked to the left and to the right. He found the section with the AR glasses. He led Suzy over there.

"Take yours off, try several of these on. Make it seem like you are interested in trading your old glasses for these new ones. After that, put yours back on and walk over to the Genius Bar.

When you get there, tell them you have a screw loose and ask to borrow their special little screwdriver. Tighten the screw, then compliment the person next to you on something. Their watch, phone, hair, anything. While you're doing that, take the screwdriver and put it in the back pocket of your sexy black jeans, then walk on out the store."

"My sexy black jeans? Do you want me to get caught? Nothing fits in those pockets. I'll use my bag."

Evan sat back quietly and watched as Suzy went to work. He didn't say a word until she had left the store and was back out in the street.

"You are such a badass Suzy."

"Here I was thinking you were going to get me into some real trouble," she laughed.

"Who's to say that I won't? I got to run now, but some other time? For real, not here. Let me take you out."

"Give me your number and we'll see. I don't know if I should trust myself around you."

"I don't trust myself around me. Be seeing you, Suzy."

Evan took the headset off and tossed it on the couch next to him. Paolo gave him the look all men do after a performance like that. Envy. He liked to explain that it was a skill like anything else. You just need to work at it and lose your fear of failure, but Paolo wasn't paying him for pickup lessons. He was paying for the psychological keys to the platform.

"There's three things to making that work. The first is the match. I picked Suzy because her profile pic was the most telling. Her outward appearance indicates a personality type that I am very compatible with. She likes bad boys that pursue her. I'm a bad boy that likes to chase girls. We have a very superficial chemistry. The second is the mission. I gave her a reason to stay in and work with me. The third was the push. I probably didn't need to, but that moment with the glamour effect and the subliminal messaging sealed the deal. I don't want to toot my own horn, but the icing on the cake was dialing down the risk. She got the rush of anticipation, but then could follow through because she was stealing a tool and not a $1500 gadget."

"And you got yourself a date. You ever get sick of your smug self?"

"I haven't yet, and we'll see if she messages me. Anyway, you and your pals need to figure out how to turn those three things into automated processes. Get that down and you'll have that monster you keep talking about."

14. THE RETRADE

They were at Rabbit's house in Hancock Park. Ivy climbed the brick walls surrounding his yard. It was Paolo's first time there. He could tell from the size of the trees and the thick roots on the shrubs that this was an old yard, maintained and loved for decades. They sat on his back patio. Dull stucco tiles mixed with brightly painted Spanish ones. A hummingbird darted through the late April flowers. The place was entirely out of character with the man he knew.

"Because you are wondering, this house had been in Diana's family since the thirties. It was the only thing I didn't want in the divorce."

"It's a lovely prize nonetheless."

"I'd prefer the dog."

Kendra walked over from the far edge of the yard. She picked up the pitcher of lemonade and poured herself an icy glass.

"So, you've cracked it?" Rabbit asked.

"You saw the video," she said, stirring sugar into her glass.

"Yes, Evan and Suzy rob the Apple store." Rabbit rolled his eyes. "I saw a player playing someone who wanted to be played."

"What do you think the point of Peared is?" Paolo shot back.

"Let's hear it Paolo. Rabbit, please let the man work. I'm not playing referee today."

"We've been approaching Peared the wrong way. We've either built a game that's an open-ended world, or we've built a tool and assumed its utility would be obvious. *Grand Theft Auto* or a telephone. Marketing is positioning it as a utility. Travel Together with Peared. Travel where? Travel for what? We've given people too much and they don't know what to do with it."

"You can do anything with it," Rabbit said.

"And no one is doing anything with it," Paolo continued. "Sometimes a product needs a narrower definition. Peared needs structure, guidance. What you saw with Evan and Suzy was an idealized version of that, but it's also a blueprint. We need to retool the entire experience as a game."

"That's going to cost me money," Rabbit grumbled.

"It's already cost us money," Kendra shot back.

"What are you proposing?" Rabbit asked.

"Mission, match, push. Just like I told you in my email. For the mission, I want to start with scavenger hunts. We define the goal. We award the prizes. I need data, so I need to test. I need a friendly construct in which to do it. I'm running a massive social experiment to figure out how to get people to manipulate each other in an open world. I can't be matching people, throwing out hints, and pushing them with psychological tricks without a good cover story. Once we understand how to pair people up and how to push them when momentum stalls out, we'll let people create their own missions. Start as a game and go back to a utility later," Paolo said.

"What do you need from us?" Rabbit asked.

"I need Sonny to build us a mission engine. I need a prize pool. We can program the missions at NAM. The match engine is all us. We'll have to dust off some of our dating site algos and start buying third party data on our users. I need to teach our AI how to do what Evan did. The match is the most important part of this. We need to put compatible alphas with betas. That's not as simple as you think. People are complex objects. Brains and brawn. Doers and thinkers. Voyeurs and exhibitionists. It will take time to program that."

"The push will be tricky," Paolo continued. "I don't know how much we'll need it, and I'm not sure how to employ it, but we'll need those glamour effects to dazzle people over the edge. Testing will tell us what is right."

"Thanks Paolo. I never doubted you. Rabbit, we need to talk money here. My people are pulling a lot more weight than we intended. NAM's job was to take a working engine, make it brutally efficient, and wring as many miles out of it as possible. You didn't give us a working engine, but we have the fixes you need. The way I see it, we hold your future in our hands," Kendra said.

Rabbit looked across the table at Kendra. She sipped her lemonade, her sandal tapping away on the tile. Kendra and Paolo had been running a two-man game on him. He wasn't surprised; in fact, he was prepared. What he couldn't figure out was if they were shaking him down or just worried about dead money. Rabbit paid NAM a percentage of all the revenue it earned. Peared had been live for a couple months and made a measly $20k. NAM's split would barely cover a week's worth of employee lunches.

"How much money have you put into Peared so far?" Rabbit asked.

"Close to $2 million. Double what I expected." Kendra answered.

"That's a big number, but not huge for a company like yours."

"True, but products usually show a pulse by now. All yours has done is sucked money out my pockets."

While Kendra and Paolo were clearly talented, making Peared go was still a roll of the dice. He figured they would need to go in another $2 to $3 million before this turned around or they decided to cut bait. If Paolo was wrong about this mission, match, and push approach, he needed Kendra to stick with Peared. He couldn't have them walk away.

The right play here was making them whole. They needed to be less worried about money spent and more worried about future earnings.

"What do you want, Kendra? I'm not negotiating against myself here."

"We are doing more work, we should get a bigger cut. Bump rev share up to 40%."

Rabbit nearly spit his lemonade out. Asking to go from 30 to 40% was ludicrous. He had his own expenses to cover. Agreeing to that would kill his future profits.

"Kendra, if I give you 40% then I won't make a dime on Peared. Be reasonable."

"What do you think is reasonable?"

"Well, you put more work in than you bargained for, but once you get that engine humming you go back to business as usual. Your costs drop, the machines take on more of the job, margins increase. Don't get greedy here. You say you've put in twice as much money as you expected. Let me cover that."

"My ask was a 40% rev share and you are offering me a million? You understand the difference there? Going to 40% will be worth a million plus a month once we get this to scale."

"It's also a deal breaker, Kendra. Your complaint is that getting Peared going cost more than you expected. I'm offering to make you whole. Don't shake me down. I don't think you want us leaving, then word getting out why."

"Make me whole now and you cover any cost overruns until we are back on budget."

"Send me the budget, let me look at it, and as long as the numbers are reasonable, I can do that. Do we have a deal?"

"Deal."

Rabbit had sat across the table from Kendra many times. He had never experienced anything like that before. Sure, early estimates were sometimes off, and deals needed to be tweaked, but that was an ill-considered cash grab. It was out of character for her. She must be under more pressure than he thought. At least she came to her senses.

He didn't like the idea of paying a couple million out of pocket, but there was no fucking way he was going to give up future earnings. Paolo had cracked the code, and they were going to break through soon. Once everyone started earning, this would all smooth over.

Money is a great deodorant.

15. TECH BEAT LA

Rabbit scanned the lobby full of laminated badges, plastic smiles, and overpriced suits. At this point, he could navigate it on autopilot. Eye contact, firm handshakes, and promises of drinks later. He made his way to registration, and stepped into the line labeled T-Z.

"Rabbit Wilson." He passed a card across the counter. Behind it, a kid wore the cheap and cheery mask of the service industry. He probably drove for Uber this morning, clocked into the event, and then would cater waiter an afterparty. Rabbit heard that a lot of the staff do it that way. Three day shows, eighteen-hour days, nothing but hustle. He looked at the kid a little more closely; he was late twenties, maybe early thirties. Hardly a kid. In the old days, he'd be running a team somewhere. Software had eaten his future.

"Here you are, Mr. Wilson."

"Gold? I'm not speaking or an organizer."

"It's Tech Beat's way of saying thanks for ten years."

Ten fucking years of this? Rabbit shook his head and walked away. He skipped the swag line. Now that his nieces and nephews were older, none of them wanted branded backpacks and light up keychains. What used to be cool was now gauche. He understood. He used to find this cool too.

He thought about his brother up in Hibbing. Stephen had quit his job, put on ten pounds and quickly settled into the comfortable life of early retirement. While Rabbit was running circles around LA trying to prove them all wrong, Stevie was building his cabin and hunting for an old wooden motorboat to restore. A part of Rabbit envied his brother's lack of drive, his contentment with a life well lived. Rabbit wasn't wired that way; he'd always been hungry. His outsized appetite put him on the outside more often than not, but there was nothing he could do about it. We are who we are. Just as Bear needed to disappear into himself, Rabbit needed to prove himself above everyone who had cast him aside.

Rabbit had only one reason for being here, to let everyone know that he was still standing. It had been a year since he walked out on Smash House, and Peared still had a long way to go. While the town was largely behind Ka$ia, he still had friends in the business. He had plenty of enemies too. No matter which side people stood on, they needed to see that Rabbit was making moves and that the best was yet to come.

He checked the speaker list; mercifully, Ka$ia was not on it. He assumed the organizers had tired of hearing the same story. She'd never turn this gig down. Scanning the lineup, he ran across a familiar name, Frank Meyers. They had bumped into each other over the years—the first few times were beyond awkward, but it had gotten to the point where neither talked about what had happened.

Rabbit made a note to find him later. First, it would be good to be seen chatting with Frank in public. People would notice that water was under that bridge. Second, he wanted to see if Frank had knives out for him. Someone had spiked that PR blitz, and he still needed a scalp.

"Rabbit, can I catch you for a moment?" Walt Jacobsen waddled on over to him.

Walt was a pioneer in the world of visual effects. The man invented CGI dinosaurs. Over the years he burnt out on movie making and fell in with the local tech community. The Tech Beat show was his baby.

"Walt buddy, good to see you."

"You too Rabbit. I was wondering if you could do me a favor. We had someone drop out of our 11 o'clock roundtable. Could an old hand like yourself take the seat?"

"What's the topic?"

"Trends for 2025. Should be an easy one. I've got a cheat sheet prepped."

"You can count on me, Walt. Do me a favor though, remember this next year. I want that keynote."

"You'll need to have quite the year to make keynote, but I'll definitely slot you as a speaker. Thanks buddy."

"Sure, pal."

Rabbit sat in the back of a darkened hall working his iPhone. He tried to tune the conference blather out. The last two kids on stage had trotted out the same tired tropes of disruption and transformation. The first was a vending machine company, the second was pitching a desktop yogurt maker. A desktop fucking yogurt maker.

Tech Beat LA was as much a debutante ball as it was a trade show. The sons and daughters of wealthy Angelenos were shipped up to Stanford, spent a couple years working in the Valley and then came back here to be crowned as future titans of industry.

Walt's email came in with the cheat sheet, room, and participant list. He was in the big room and Frank Meyers was on the panel. Well, look at that. Either the fates had ordained this, or Walt was a lot craftier than he let on. Rabbit got up and left the hall. He had an hour to get his shit together.

At 10:45 he walked into the green room. It was a four-person panel. He saw Debbie Lau working her phone and gave her a nod. Trish Haverstrom had not arrived yet. That left Frank sitting in a corner eating an everything bagel slathered in a pink schmear.

He had sharpened up his glasses. Rabbit guessed those frames cost three grand. That stupid goatee was still there, though. Rabbit never had to worry about thinning hair, but if he had, he wouldn't compensate by hanging a bunch of it off his mouth.

"Had I known," Rabbit said sitting opposite him.

"You still would have done it," Frank finished.

"I would, but I would have checked with you first. Walt didn't give me the lineup until afterwards."

"Walt's an ass that way. He's looking for fireworks. Just so you know, it wasn't me. I didn't spike your launch."

"I never suspected."

"Don't play dumb. Em and I have mutual friends. She called me the day after launch, bullshit to the moon. Whatever history we have, I'd never cross her. I might need her someday. That's the thing about this town. It's all the same people, Rabbit. You never realized that. It's why your circle keeps getting smaller, and mine keeps growing. Had you made friends, treated people a certain way, they'd be here for you now when you need it most. Instead, you are out in the wilderness, hiding in Kendra's shadows and running black ops out of NAM. That's a long way from home Rabbit, a long way. Anyway, no hard feelings. I don't want fireworks. Let's get up there, play nice, and hug it out on stage."

"Hug it out?" Rabbit stared across at Frank. He tried to look him in the eye, but the crumbs in his goatee were just too much.

"Anger burns hot, but quick. Forgiveness I've come to find, is a deeper, more sustaining energy."

Frank Meyers had gone new age. Rabbit would have to find out the name of his guru and send him a Christmas card.

While he wasn't one to let a smug lecture go unanswered, it seemed a fair trade, all things considered. Hug it out, show everyone there was no hard feelings. There were a million different ways this could have gone. This was easily the best. Besides, he was in a giving mood. Paolo was reporting success with some of his early tests.

16. THE ILLEGITIMATE FIREMEN OF INSTAGRAM

Em furrowed her brow and pulled her hair into a ponytail. In front of her were dozens of concepts neatly arranged on a table. They were grouped into broad ideas for missions like discover, rescue, and race. Some were straight ahead, while others took an absurdist twist.

She picked up a vision board with beefcake guys, bachelorettes, and a description which read: "The Illegitimate Fireman of Instagram have invaded. Round them up before their body heat burns the whole city down."

So, this is what it had come to, sexist Farmville shit. She picked up another: "A pot of gold awaits at the end of the rainbow. Discover it and earn a spin on the Fortune Wheel."

Great, let's go for gullible gamblers.

Thank God these were just pitches and they hadn't paid for these concepts. She fired off a quick email. Hard pass. Tone deaf.

The thing was that the missions were right, but the packaging was wrong. If Peared was going to make it, and that was a big IF in her mind now, they'd need to do it in a way where they could grow back into their original positioning. Everything she believed and felt about the service remained true. Peared needed to promote equality and team work between

Hands and Eyes. It needed to be viewed as a mind-blowing tool that allowed you to look at the world through another person's eyes.

How to get there was the challenge.

They had to get the ball rolling somewhere. She walked over to another table. It played right down the middle. Earn badges and unlock status. Win tickets to concerts. Limited edition gear. Sure, they were recycled quests from old apps, but they had worked before. Peared needed to find a pulse, and unlike the Illegitimate Fireman, partnering with Adidas and The Voice gave them an air of credibility.

With Travel Together, Em thought she had a surefire campaign. In her mind, the product was legless. They couldn't afford to make that mistake again. It was time for marketing to push the burden back on the product. Either Paolo and Sonny delivered, or she'd start filling her calendar with new clients.

17. MATCHMAKERS

Paolo stood in his office and watched his team hard at work. He saw Carlos the receptionist bent over chatting with Diana, their AI lead. One had an EQ off the charts, the other a genius IQ. Between them was a split screen monitor. They were eavesdropping on a Peared session. The rest of the group were in various stages of spying. Some were plotting to pair people together based on a combination of data and intuition. Others were testing subtle pushes into missions to keep pairs working together. The final group were performing session replays, searching for clues to what made good matches.

While an AI would ultimately perform all of these jobs, they had a long way to go before getting there. So much of what they were trying to manufacture was in the soft skills. Verbal cues, body language, and pacing. Machines could be taught what those meant, but they couldn't identify them on their own. That was still a job for people.

None of this would be possible if they followed the Silicon Valley Code, but FriendZone rules allowed it. The terms and conditions were designed so that Peared and its associated vendors had the right to monitor active sessions in order to improve the overall quality of the service. The phrase "overall quality of the service" was vague enough that it could mean anything, and so was "monitoring active sessions."

Rabbit's rules of engagement were to simply not break any local laws. Most of the world did not have the protections that Europe and the US had, so Paolo was free to snoop and manipulate as he saw fit. The launch of missions had given them some traction. After experimenting with prizes, they discovered that topping up cellphones played big overseas. He found the poorest countries where unemployment was high, technology was cheap, and people had time to kill. He flooded those markets with missions to earn free airtime, timing marketing to days where carriers launched bonus promotions like double data.

Peared started shooting up the international app charts. More importantly, it was accumulating the data needed to refine the service into a success.

Paolo knew that many people had ethical problems with his approach. He simply did not care. All of humanity was some form of manipulation from time immemorial. The strongest hunter manipulated the tribe. Whomever claimed to speak for God manipulated the nation. Now manipulation was digital. The methods had changed, but the relationship had not. People needed to be led.

Strength no longer ruled people, nor did belief in God. Attention now ruled people.

Paolo had the ability to capture people's attention because he could think deeply about systems. He understood machines, he understood people, and he had an intimate understanding of the relationship between people and their machines. Most importantly, Paolo was an obsessive thinker. His self-worth was tied to the difficulty of the problem that he was working on. Money mattered, and power did too, but it was critical that he fed his brain with something so demanding that it consumed the entirety of him. If he didn't have that, the doubts and boredom of everyday life ate him from the inside out. Peared was now his only waking thought.

He didn't care what he was doing to others because it was the only way to protect him from himself.

18. CURRENTS

A Google alert for Peared hit Em's screen. A teenaged boy in Mumbai had drowned attempting to reach an island. There had been a bridge there, but it was recently torn down so that it could be replaced by a larger road. The boy's family was blaming Peared for sending him out there on a mission. She pulled Rabbit aside.

"Have you seen this?" she asked, holding her phone, being careful not to forward it to him.

"No. Has anyone contacted us about it?"

"I'm just seeing it now. NAM handles care. It's all automated. There could be something in their queue. If they called headquarters, someone would have passed that message along."

They walked over to reception. No calls from India had come in.

"What do you want to do about it?" she asked.

"First of all, let's see if we had a mission out there. If we did, we need to turn it off ASAP, after that this is Paolo's problem."

"How is it Paolo's problem?"

"He manages and operates the service. He programs the missions. We are just a technology platform. He is legally liable as the operator."

"Hold on. He's liable?"

"Why do you think NAM exists?"

"I figured they were cheaper, and you didn't wan. many people."

"Well yes, there's both of those, but liability protectic added bonus. It's complicated, but at the end of the day we u run Peared. They do. It's Paolo's problem."

"You can't walk away from this Rabbit," Em said.

"I'm not, but I'm also assigning it to the proper party. Paolo needs to look into this and come back with a conclusion, then he needs to present us with options."

"Maybe that works from a legal standpoint, but from a PR perspective it's a fucking nightmare. No one is going to care about this abstraction, and I'm not going to be the face of a company that works this way."

"I didn't ask you to be the face. I asked you to design an image. Nothing here has gone out in your name. It's gone out in mine."

"Hey dipshit, you know what's a bad image? Getting branded as a murderer, then not responding to a grieving family."

"I didn't say I wouldn't respond, but I need facts first. That kid could have gone out there to drink and smoke weed. Do us all a favor, craft a response in case there's more to this than a reporter quoting a shocked mother grasping at straws."

Em burnt furiously inside as she watched Rabbit walk away. So that's how it was. Build walls, protect yourself, and don't show any emotion other than annoyance. Some kid could be dead because of Peared and Rabbit was fine waiting on a report to find out. He was also ready to pin it on Paolo from the start. Maybe she was jumping the gun, but one thing was clear. Rabbit was a fucking asshole.

19. PEP TALK

Paolo looked at his ink-smeared palm. After trying apps, reminders, and paper lists, his palm ended up being his most trusted organizer. It was impossible to lose, and a quick turn of the wrist showed everything left to do. He licked his opposite thumb and erased Mumbai from his skin. Peared was not running missions to that island. Users alerted the app the bridge was out, and the system removed the mission, exactly according to protocol.

It was one less thing for Paolo to worry about. Death would have been a major bummer and thrown the team into chaos. As it was, Paolo could barely keep up with his new responsibilities. Three months after launch, Peared was up to five million users and his group had grown to over forty people. He'd been comfortable being a specialist, the guy they called in to crack the toughest nuts. Now, they wanted him to shift gears and keep track of everything. At times he felt like he was drowning.

They were outgrowing their wing on the Vampire Floor. While there was now fresh coffee in the morning, the night shift was getting upset at the sprawling day timers. Every day there'd be a new set of angry notes pinned to his command tent. Kendra was going to move the team somewhere soon. She was also getting him a capable number two. He desperately needed an experienced manager to oversee the day-to-day. Paolo belonged out on the bleeding edge. He was tasked with growth, but he spent his time worrying who was on pager duty.

His phone buzzed. It was Rabbit; Paolo had forgotten to call him.

"Paolo here."

"Am I going to get a report on Mumbai?"

"Sorry. I've had a lot going on. We are clear there."

"I figured as much. Had someone died you would have cal. me. You sound stressed. Having trouble keeping up?"

"A bit. How do you do it?"

"At this point it's second nature. Don't worry, you'll get there. Managing is an acquired skill—it's repetition and experience. Accumulated wisdom. No one starts out good at it. You'll grow up quick."

"Why would I want to become a manager?"

"You'll need it when you become one of us Paolo. I'm sure there's an idea somewhere inside of you. If not, I'm sure you have that drive to create something for yourself. You're too smart not to."

"Thanks Rabbit. I appreciate the compliment."

"I don't usually go easy on people, but you sound like you could use it. You remind me of myself Paolo. The younger me, the one that was good, not the ass I am now. This may seem a little overwhelming, but you have what it takes. What is about to happen at Peared—what you are going to make happen—it's going to change everything about you for the better. You will be tested in ways you never imagined. You will develop skills you never dreamed possible. When it's over, you'll have the confidence to do anything in the world. You already have the smarts."

"It doesn't feel that way."

"That's because you are in it. It will get dark for sure. There will be times when you won't feel human, but keep pushing through and you'll get there. You feel better? I can keep going with this speech if you need more. Whatever it takes to keep our star going."

"Thanks Rabbit. I'm good."

"Anytime Paolo. I've been in some bad shit. There were times when I could have used someone who understood. If you find yourself there, let me know. I'm here for you."

"I will."

20. A BOTTOM

It was their first time in the wooden hut since the Travel Together pitch. Em sat on a toadstool watching the projected stream at her feet. Rabbit had his back to her. He was inspecting the pile of stuffies, looking for flies, mildew or some excuse to pitch them in the trash. The pile had grown since he lay Yosemite's head down. At some point a company tradition would become a health hazard, but today was not that day. He turned and sat. Em spoke.

"Rabbit, I've been doing some digging and I finally got to the bottom of the press blacklist. It wasn't Frank, it wasn't Ka$ia— it was you, Rabbit."

"Me? Why would I spike my launch PR?"

"Because you held out on me. Now we are going to talk about Nadia Camiso."

The name punched him in the gut. His jaw slackened, and his face went to the floor. While his eyes fixated on the stream, they were not there. He was traveling within himself, backwards to a terrible place. Em patiently waited him out, her grey eyes never wavering. After a long silence, he began pinching his pant leg, pulling his fingers down the crease line over and over. Finally, Em had enough. If he was going to talk, now was it.

"Rabbit."

"I can't talk about her," He squeezed his leg, fingers digging into his thigh.

Em held firm. "We have no future unless you do."

"We met once before the affair. It was a fundraiser at Hank impson's place in Bel Air. That was the first time Diana met Jason as well. Of course, they would meet plenty more times."

"When did you start texting?"

"One night Jason left the inside security cameras on. Diana came over to their house. I'm not sure where Nadia was, but she was watching. She started sending me screencaps, calling my wife a whore, a homewrecker."

"What did you do?"

"I started in on Nadia. I called her a pervert, a voyeur, said she was getting off on it. I said their bedroom kink was ruining my marriage and how fucking dare she send pics."

"And?"

"Em, I can't. If I say anymore, I'm opening myself up to all sorts of sexual harassment exposure here. We can't be talking about this."

"We can, and we will." Em pushed him. "I already know the story Rabbit. I just want to hear your side of it."

"She said I was probably hard and itching for her to send the next one. I wasn't. I was revolted. Sick to my stomach."

"Why were you attacking Nadia?"

"She was in my line of sight." Rabbit squirmed in his seat. "The others weren't."

"So, what happened next?"

"Nadia had a way with words. She pushed buttons. What I learned was that there was a hole inside of her that could never be filled. She gave it right back to me and we were off to the races. Just like that, our texts turned toxic. We were using the drama we created as some sick way to cope with what was really happening. Cathartic flagellation. It got deep. We went way over the line. Mutually abusive. We dropped some heavy psych bombs on each other. She didn't come back."

"People asked you to stop."

"They did." Rabbit stood unable to sit still any lo. wanted to pace, but the small hut had him penned in. He Em, holding his hands, unsure what to do with them. "Frienc hers sat us down. We promised to, but I couldn't control myse. Neither could she."

"Then after the divorce, you dropped her cold."

"I didn't need her anymore. Our...our thing was a byproduct of their affair. When that ended, our thing died." He turned away from Em, hand on a beam.

"She didn't see it that way."

"I tried. I sat down with her and tried to explain. I didn't run from her. I closed it the right way. Em, you have to understand that relationship was so ugly, so bare and brutal, that there was no other direction it could take. We were monsters."

"Did you kill her?"

"That's a loaded question. I wasn't the person I should have been, but this would have never happened if her husband and my wife hadn't cheated on us. This would have never happened with anyone other than Nadia. That was not something I went looking for."

"Her friends blame you Rabbit. They think that your words are dangerous and that you need to be silenced."

"I don't know what the fuck happened with Nadia. It was like two people just gave in to their worst. And it was two people Em. I have screenshots. If this ever comes out, I'm playing victim. She put a mind fuck on me you wouldn't believe."

Knowing that Rabbit may never open himself like this again, Em went deeper, searching for a moral absolute at the center of this man. "Yet you're still standing. In fact, you are the sole owner of a company that controls people. She committed suicide. Are you in therapy?"

73

"I was."

"Was?"

"It stopped being helpful."

"I don't know if I can stay on Rabbit. What else is inside of you?"

"There's nothing else. Frank and Nadia are all the skeletons that you'll find."

"I don't mean your past. I mean what's inside of you?"

"I wish I knew Em."

He got up and left the hut. Em watched him walk away. Rabbit wasn't amoral—the incident clearly hurt him—but he wasn't contrite either. He had tried to put out fire with gasoline. In hindsight, he knew that was a mistake, but Em thought he was just as likely to do it again. His past was a liability, but his inability to manage rejection was the real ticking time bomb. Would he ever be capable of asking for help, or would he continue to turn his back after every bad move?

She could start filling her calendar and never look back. He had opened up to her though. His story matched what she was told. She didn't think he was holding back. The real challenge here was not marketing Peared, it was managing Rabbit. The question was, did she want it?

Probably not. She never enjoyed masochism.

21. OFFICE PARTY

The DJ took a break from the music, and Rabbit stepped onto the makeshift stage in the middle of their office. They were celebrating two milestones: Peared's 25th million download and hitting 500,000 concurrent pairs. Both were huge accomplishments for a product that had struggled out of the gate just six months earlier. They were now the number one app in eight different countries. Peared scavenger hunts were the hottest activity in India, Colombia, and the Philippines. Even better, Peared was transitioning from a toy to a tool.

Em gathered Sonny and Paolo in the far corner of the office. More than anyone, the three of them were responsible for tonight's success and they barely knew each other. She suspected that was intentional. Rabbit didn't like office alliances. He didn't like questioning. His playbook was to isolate employees, then push them hard to get what he wanted. Either they responded to his tactics or he disposed of them.

While everyone knew the Frank Meyers story, Sonny and Paolo didn't know about Nadia Camiso, or the hostile work environment claims at Smash House. None of those were a smoking gun, but they added up to a troubling pattern. Left alone, Rabbit went too far.

Peared was now a rocket ship and success overwhelmed Em's instincts to walk away. After weeks of turning Rabbit down, she finally accepted his offer and came on board as Chief Marketing Officer. Tasked with building out the marketing department, she was ready to reach into her network to fill positions, but first needed to unite with Paolo and Sonny. As allies they could keep Rabbit under control. As allies they could protect their stock options.

"All I am saying is that he doesn't work like most people. You need to be on your toes and we need to be united," Em said as she led them into a conference room away from prying eyes.

"You don't trust him?" Sonny asked.

"Look, he's brilliant and he's determined. I trust him 99% of the time, the thing is, no one is perfect. Rabbit doesn't let people in. He doesn't trust anyone enough to hear he's wrong. When he gets into trouble that other 1% of the time it's because no one's there to pull him back."

Realizing this wasn't a casual conversation, Paolo placed his drink on the table and gave her his full attention. "And you're suggesting the three of us pull him back?"

"Something like that. If the three of us are in contact, if we keep in touch, and we present a united front, we can steer Rabbit away from trouble. I'm sure you've all felt lonely in this job, but you haven't said anything about it. You've just soldiered on because you have high expectations for yourselves. I'm like that too. He picks people like us on purpose, so that he can run the show his way. We need to be a little smarter than him. This isn't going to be some big drama show. All we have to do is anticipate his blind spots and solve those problems before he mucks them up."

Sonny looked past Em, across the office, towards the stage where Rabbit was. "If that's all you are asking, I have no problem tackling issues before he's aware of them," Sonny said.

"I'm in as well," Paolo said.

Em looked at Paolo and then Sonny. "Good, let's keep Rabbit from shooting himself and Peared in the foot. You need anything involving him, you come to me. I understand how he thinks, and I'll tell you how to handle him."

22. FUTURE TIME

Paolo lived in the future. Hitting milestones rarely mattered to him. They'd already been calculated into his equations, assumed and absorbed. Besides, there was always another problem set to be solved. He didn't care about 500,000 concurrent pairs or all-time highs because he had to figure out how to double, then triple, those records.

One number absolutely mattered though. It was more the color than the number.

The Peared account was finally in the black.

He sat alone in his new office on the fourth floor and peeled the seal off of a Macallan 18. He uncorked it, shut his eyes, and inhaled the deep aroma.

Kendra had given it to him at the start of this engagement. Since then, it sat on his bookshelf waiting for their first profitable week. He'd wondered at times if they would hit it, but they had. The team had decoded human behavior, asked their AI the right questions, and then fed a playbook back into the AI.

There were no more spook sessions with people peering in on people. They were past that. The growth everyone back-slapped themselves over happened because Paolo's team had fully automated the mission, match, and push process. Once they automated it, they brought it to scale. Every user was now being guided by a machine that would only get better over time.

The amber gold swirled around his glass. He held off his first taste, teasing himself, delaying the gratification until he could wait no longer. Then there was the burn followed by the smooth heat.

He relaxed for the first time in forever. He'd risked so much on Peared. It was a more dangerous gamble than he was comfortable with, but it was also the most powerful product he had ever seen. At times he doubted his ability to tame the beast, but he never gave up. Now, the pressure was off, and they could go back to their usual cadence of efficiency above all.

Most of the products they managed maxed out a certain point. Markets are only so big, and inevitably a product reaches a point where it can't acquire additional customers without losing money. When that happens, you top out, and the only thing left to do is squeeze blood from a stone.

Peared wasn't like other products. It didn't have a ceiling. It was for everyone. What encouraged him most was that regulars were switching over from missions to freestyle mode. After a while, Eyes found it normal to hire Hands to act as their real-life avatars. Can't make it to a wedding? RSVP and send someone in your place. Want to get away? Microvacation. Fire up the treadmill, put VR glasses on and stroll the Champs Elysées while at the gym. It took a bit, but people were becoming comfortable with teleportation as an actual thing instead of a novel two-person game. With visas so tough, Paolo felt it was only a matter of time before people hid behind Hands to take jobs in other countries. Would employers even mind? After all, two heads are better than one.

At some point in time, there was only one television station in the world. There was only one telephone company. Right now, there was only one teleportation provider and Paolo operated it. No one ever gets a chance like that. Paolo had to get it out to as many people as he could as fast as he could before competition sprang up. There was an entire world for the taking, ready for real transformation. Paolo had turned Peared from a confusing, awkward experience no one would use to the brink of the mainstream success. What would happen once it really broke through? He took a second sip of scotch and tried to calm his runaway mind. Sleep would be difficult tonight. He'd need to tranquilize himself, either booze or pills, but his brain would have to be subdued.

He hoped that profitability meant that Rabbit and Kendra would back off and let him work. He had to start building out some trade secrets to hold over them. After Kendra had failed to take a bigger cut out of Rabbit's end, she approached him trying to trade his earn out for stock options. He turned her down but suspected that wasn't the end of it. She was starting to think very short term. It made Paolo wonder if her future at NAM was tied to turning Peared into a major account. Trouble for Kendra was bad news for him. She gave him executive perks like free corporate housing, an assistant, and most importantly, NAM sponsored his green card application. While Paolo was worthy of some of those, others were because of their long history to-gether. Whether she stayed or went, he needed to make himself untouchable until he got his green card. After that, all bets were off.

23. A HYPOTHETICAL

Paolo was on his third Macallan when his phone rang. It was Kendra. He corked the bottle and put it back on the shelf. He'd get himself in trouble if he finished this one and then absently poured a fourth.

"Paolo here."

A noisy buzz filled the background on the other line. After a moment Kendra cut above the din. "Congratulations are in order. I hope you are enjoying your first profitable week."

"Thank you. I'm heading out with the team for dinner."

"Well, I won't keep you too long. Malcolm and I just had the most interesting conversation. Can I share it with you?"

Paolo looked out the window. He could see traffic backing up in the distance. He was supposed to be in Palo Alto in thirty minutes. If he didn't leave now, the commute would be impossible. Then again, he was the boss, they could wait. He rubbed his brow, accepting the necessity of this call. We all got to serve.

Paolo sat on the edge of his desk, watching as the cleaning crew got off the elevator. "Of course, Kendra."

"Well, we are out at dinner and right in the middle of it, Malcolm's clients need to leave for an emergency. We've got four bottles of bubbly open and a raw seafood tower that can feed ten people, only no one to share it with."

Paolo sighed. He'd had a few of these calls from Kendra before. She has too much to drink and thinks that what comes next will change the world.

"So, Malcolm and I start this game we like to play where we try to one up each other with crazy ideas. Usually it's stupid shit, but Malcolm has one that stops me dead in my tracks. You ready for this?"

"I'm seated Kendra."

"You know how they get drones to synch up and move together like a swarm?"

"I've seen them, yes."

"What if we could do that with people?"

Paolo stood. "With Peared?"

"Yes. With Peared. Could we do it?"

He took a sip and thought for a moment. "I don't know. I've never even considered it."

"Hypothetically?"

"Hypothetically, we could form impromptu gangs. I'd create centaurs to do it."

"What's a centaur?" Kendra asked over the noise of dinner service.

"Maybe it's better we speak when we are both sober. I've had a few. You are out in Vegas."

"Worried you'll say something you regret? Don't be nervous Paolo, you can share your secret thoughts with me. Now tell me, what's a centaur?"

"Find a quieter place Kendra. I need your full attention for this."

"You're pulling me away from Malcolm," she laughed. "He won't like that. I hope this is good."

After a few minutes, a much quieter Kendra returned. "Is my favorite employee still on the line? I found a little nook off the reception area, just like you asked."

"I'm here Kendra. Ready?"

"Give it to me, Paolo."

Paolo finished the last of his drink, placed the glass tumbler on his desk and began to walk in circles around his office. "Ok, a centaur is a combination of humans and AI. AI's are really good at getting answers, but terrible at asking questions. People are really good at asking questions. You put them together as a team and you have a centaur that's greater than the sum of the parts."

"Don't we have that right now? Hands, Eyes, and AI all together."

He stopped and stared out at traffic trying to think of how to best explain the difference. "Sort of. Right now, the AI's job is to figure out who to invite to dinner, what to serve, and every so often it changes the mood at the table. What it's not doing is sitting down and eating. With a gang, you need a much more active AI. It has to be at the table or in this case, out in the field. However, there's no way an AI could manage a gang. It's too chaotic and people answer to leaders, not machines."

"So true Paolo. By the way, you are growing into your new role quite nicely. Turning into a real leader yourself. Don't think I haven't noticed."

"Thanks, but let's focus Kendra." Paolo began walking again. "Say you wanted a hundred-person centaur gang to show up at a protest. It would look like this. We'd have a command hierarchy somewhere. One boss to manage ten Eyes. Unlike regular Peared, each set of Eyes would operate ten pairs of Hands. The AI's would be augmenting the Eyes. They'd scan the crowd to read emotions, identify people likely to act a certain way, monitor reactions to what was being said."

"So, we are creating Super Eyes?" Kendra asked.

"In a manner of speaking, yes. With that sort of information, the Eyes could evaluate what they see and tell the Hands how to act. Say there's a really charismatic speaker on the platform. The AI could dig up counterpoints to that speaker. It could spread misinformation. It could break fake news. Once that news was out there, you could trigger your Hands to amplify it. Start chanting, rush towards the stage, shout down people and change the mood. People are fickle, crowds can turn. If that failed, well then you start exploiting the frustration of your Hands. Get them worked up and turn them to violence. A hundred angry men could clear a two-thousand-person crowd really quick. Start beating those in front and the back will flee."

"Why do you men always turn to violence? Why couldn't this be about flash mobs or dance troupes?"

Paolo eyed the Macallan, but thought better of it. "Because I doubt that's what you and Malcolm had in mind."

"Well Malcolm and I have thought up some very interesting uses for Peared. Maybe you'll find out about them one day. Anyways, sorry for interrupting. You were beating people up with AI centaurs."

Paolo sighed, realizing how quickly he had turned Peared dark. "I'm almost done. For the last part, you need to create a strong process inside your centaur. Process is as critical as your people and AIs. Skilled operators, a charismatic leader, AIs trained to perform very specialized tasks. You'd need to create the right matches with your Hands. You'd have to feed them very strong incentives. This isn't something you just do with randoms until you got very good at it. You need to train as a team and get comfortable with the process."

"Like in the Philippines with Duerte and his men?"

"That would be the sort of testing environment we'd need. Cops fighting drug dealers. Seasoned men with an already defined mission. We could learn a lot there. Hypothetically."

"Interesting. Very interesting. Thanks for making the time

Paolo. I'd love to chat some more, but Malcolm gets so lonely without me."

"Kendra, is this a thing you are considering?"

"No, it's just a crazy idea that I wanted to run by that big brain of yours. You know, a hypothetical. Anyway, I've got to run. Thanks Paolo."

Paolo clicked his phone off. He looked out his window; the red lights of cars were jammed tight in all directions. So much for playing things close to the vest. He just gave Kendra a framework for running remote control mobs. There had to be stupid money in that sort of work, but you'd also have to be stupid to do it.

He called a Lyft. He rubbed his temple and felt the booze swirling inside. Why had Malcom asked her that question? It seemed a little too specific and given how Paolo answered it, not that crazy. He decided to research Malcolm Dubour. At the very least, it would give him something to do while stuck in traffic.

24. UNSOLICITED

Rabbit had a few offers for Peared already, but they weren't serious. Peter Thorn was different. He was a member of the Pay-Town Mafia, an early investor in FriendZone, and the head of Thorn Capital. While Thorn made plenty of small bets on new startups, he rarely bought companies others founded. He didn't need to.

Thorn Capital was also known as the Thorn Chaebol in the Valley. All its portfolio companies were tightly interconnected. Sometimes you couldn't tell where one ended and the other began. They shared campuses, they swapped executives, they negotiated purchasing deals as a block. Piss off one and you pissed them all off. Thorn preferred to build instead of buy. It ensured that his people and his culture were in a company's DNA from the start. There were exceptions of course. Sometimes the runaway growth and unlimited potential of a product made it necessary to go outside the family. FriendZone had spent billions on InstaSnap and Who's Home? While people praised CEO Marc Stetson's vision for those moves, Thorn had pulled the strings on them.

Like everyone in tech, Rabbit kept an eye on Thorn. He was simply too big not to. Rabbit viewed him as the alien leader of another planet. Nothing in the Valley made sense to him. The ideas were too fantastic and the bets too speculative. Founder worship drove him crazy. The entire thing was a cult of nerds. If forced to choose, Rabbit would be a Scientologist before he'd be some biohacking Valley burner. He at least understood L. Ron's racket.

Thorn's acquisition guy, Adam Mason, had called him over the weekend. They wanted to buy Rabbit out. $250 million cash on the barrel. No stock options, no lockup period, no need to go north and work for FriendZone. Just a clean takeout to hand Peared over and walk away.

The call came out of the blue, like a spaceship landing in his backyard. Rabbit whipsawed between shock and awe. Peared had been doing well but still hadn't broken through in America. It was clowning around in third world markets, handing out token prizes for completing missions. Most of his users were kids in their late teens with no buying power or advertiser friendly qualities. The graphics were rough, the messaging sounded like carnival barking, and the tech press still hated Rabbit. While Paolo saw real transformative potential in pockets of users, it would be a long time before Peared posed a threat to FriendZone.

Yet Peter Thorn, the man who controlled half the internet, saw it as one.

He wanted Peared, and he wanted nothing to do with Rabbit.

It was a conundrum that rubbed Rabbit the wrong way. On the one hand, an exit would show LA just what they missed out on. He could get his satisfaction and a 10X return on his inheritance in under two years. After that he could fuck off and do whatever he wanted. On the other hand, it was rejection on a larger scale. This man, the father of consumer internet, didn't want to let Rabbit into the club. He could hear it in Mason's tone. Rabbit wasn't worthy of his invention. Its proper home was up north. They thought Rabbit got lucky, when it was anything but that. Rabbit wasn't a wildcatter that struck an accidental gusher. He belonged and wasn't going to be pushed aside so easily.

Rabbit told Mason he was going to pass.

He told him the same thing the next day when Mason offered $350 million.

Just to test them, Rabbit countered with a little under half of Peared as it was for $150 million. It would stay in LA and Rabbit would run it. Rabbit wanted those assholes to come out and say that he wasn't good enough for them, that he wasn't their sort of guy. If they just said it, he'd sell the whole damn thing for $350 million.

Instead they simply passed and withdrew their previous offer.

Cowards. At least his father had been man enough to tell Rabbit he wasn't wanted.

25. CLONE CLUB

Rabbit was in his backyard picking up palm fronds. It was a disgusting late September day, six months from the last good rain. Wind kicked dirt everywhere. His gardener had come yesterday, just before the Santa Anas rolled in. He wouldn't be back for a week, so it was on Rabbit to pick up the pieces. He took a break, feeling sweat run down his back.

His phone vibrated on the patio table, edging itself between the slats, threatening to fall to the tile below. He was in no mood to talk, but he needed to put that phone somewhere before he had a cracked screen.

Frank Meyers was ringing. That was odd and worth answering.

"Hello."

"Rabbit, Frank Meyers here."

Rabbit wiped the sweat from his brow. "Hey Frank. What can I do for you?"

"I was just up in the Valley last week. Spent a lot of time on Sand Hill Road."

"Good for you."

"Not good for you."

Rabbit looked around for a glass of water. "How's that?"

"You know how VCs all chase the craze du jour? Clean tech, subscription boxes, big data, clouds."

"Yeah."

"Well Rabbit and Peared are on the menu this week. Everyone is coming for you."

"Success brings imitators. I'm not surprised." Rabbit walked inside and grabbed a bottle off his counter.

"Neither am I. I was at Thorn Capital. They want me to join the management team of a teleportation startup. I'm going to be the adult in the room."

"They tried to buy me last week. I figured this was their next move. They only want you to piss me off. If I were you Frank, I wouldn't waste my time up there. Thorn might be big, but I'm burning a lot hotter than anyone knows. Don't get in the ring."

"I appreciate the concern, but there's a tsunami of money lined up against you. It's not just Thorn. You aren't deep enough to get in the pool with the Valley."

Rabbit squeezed the water bottle in his hand, forcing it to crinkle and crumble. "I'm printing money right now. Don't think I can't hang with the best of them."

"I don't think you know what money looks like Rabbit. There's still time to sell. Adam Mason wanted you to know their offer still stands."

"Tell Mason my offer still stands. Thorn is more than welcome to invest in an LA based Peared that I run."

"Rabbit, that ain't happening. You're dirty and you know it. Swallow your pride and sell while there's still a big payday for you. If you don't accept their offer, they'll steamroll you. Don't get into a war you can't win. Sell and take your victory lap around LA. The Valley is an entirely different world. You can't beat them."

"Don't tell me what to do."

"Just offering advice, to a friend."

Rabbit laughed. "Friend? You're a competitor Frank. I'll be

gunning for you real soon."

"I'll see you around, friendo."

"Go fuck yourself Frank."

The phone slipped through his sweaty hands and landed on the tile. It caught an edge and then fell on the hard metal back. He picked it up. Still in one piece.

26. HARDER, BETTER

Paolo put his phone down. That could have gone worse. Rabbit could have asked him to invent real teleportation. Instead, he asked to make Peared an overnight success in the US. That would not be easy. In fact, he wasn't sure if Peared was going to be a success here period. They were at a disadvantage in America. They didn't have all the tools in their box. Em's launch campaign had failed. Customer protections existed. The tech press still hated them. Everyone was looking for the next boogieman. They needed to creep up on that country, not storm the gates.

He had tried arguing this with Rabbit. Peared was growing like crazy in Asia and South America. After briefly crossing into profitability, Paolo needed to staff up and Peared had gone back in the red. Meanwhile in LA, Sonny was having trouble keeping the service online. He was spinning up new servers left and right. His developers were rewriting code that didn't scale. It was all hands on deck, yet that mad man needed more.

As much as Paolo liked to think he didn't need Kendra, this was one of those times when she was invaluable. He went upstairs and was waved into her office by Kendra's Chief of Staff. The room was sparse, even by Valley standards. Kendra was nowhere to be seen. He paused, his feet deep in white shag carpeting, his eyes looking at an empty glass desk. Behind it was a high-backed white leather chair facing out the window. Kendra was nowhere to be seen.

"Paolo, what's the matter?" A voice called out from the chair, followed by the sound of nails on a glass touch screen.

"What makes you think there's a problem?"

"You used to come by just to say hello. Now you never do. Although it wouldn't kill you to." Kendra spun the chair around. She was dressed in all black, her blonde hair pulled back.

"Sorry Kendra. It's Rabbit."

"Of course, it's Rabbit. Pull up a stump and tell me what the problem is?"

Paolo grabbed one of the three smooth tree trunks from the side of her office, placed it in front of her desk and took a seat. "He needs us to own America ASAP."

"Does he now?" she asked.

"That's the latest directive."

"He's feeling the heat. Peter Thorn is coming for him, which means he's coming for us too."

Paolo drummed his hands on the wood between his legs. "Fuck."

"Yup, fuck."

"So, what do we do?"

"We do what we always do, figure out how to make money. If you make money, all your other problems are secondary or solvable."

"You know my first rule Kendra."

She spun her chair in slow rotations and recited his mantra. "Find your hits and ride them into the ground."

"America is not a hit. It's not even a deep cut on the album."

"No, and it's not a place I want us fighting for right now. We are at a severe disadvantage there." Her fingers grabbed the glass desk and brought her chair to a sudden halt. "What do you want to do?"

"I'd like to keep blowing out the markets that are working.

Brazil, Mexico, Philippines, India, etc. There's over two billion people right there. Last month we had eighty million of them. This month we have a hundred million. In another month I'll have 130. Right now, we need to hold the wheel steady while we press the gas harder."

"Was this the first time Rabbit asked to own America?"

"Yes."

"Good." She leaned back. "That gives us time. Remember, we don't get in dick measuring contests. We don't do it with our clients and we don't do it on behalf of our clients. Do this, squeeze what's working harder. Test more aggressive tactics. Get some really deep hooks into people. If someone is coming for Peared, I want us to have a wide moat around our markets. As for America, I'll give you a couple of our major account strategists to help. Who do you like working with?"

"The Sams."

"Guy Sam is free. Girl Sam is on Netflix, but I can pull her. They are going to work with you on a proposal for Rabbit. They'll cost out what it would require to break through in the US. We can't use FriendZone rules, so it will cost more. It will be a such big number that Rabbit won't have second thoughts, he'll have third thoughts. In the meantime, squeeze margins. Plow everything into growth. I want to create a short-term cash crunch so that he feels poor and backs off the US."

"Why are we acting against our client?" Paolo asked.

"Because he's thinking with the wrong organ. No one fucks Peter Thorn. Work with the Sams on something painful, but that could succeed. I think Rabbit will back down once he cools off, but if he doesn't, whatever we sell him on needs to have a chance of working. Did he define owning America?"

"No."

"Good. That's more room to maneuver. Draw up cases for one, ten, and twenty-five million users. How's everything else,

Paolo?"

"Everything else? There's nothing else Kendra. You know that."

"Find something else. Stop spending your weekends climbing rocks. You're a good-looking guy. Get out there and meet someone. The job won't save you. Like I said earlier, come by sometime just to say hi."

"Thanks."

27. WITHOUT AMERICA

Rabbit weighed the situation. This was a moment where he had to decide if he should listen to the voice inside him or to his people. The voice told him to own America. His people all said to stick to what's working. Don't fuck up a good thing.

Without America they would do well for a while, but then get eaten alive.

First, Peared would be left out of the conversation. Whenever anyone talked about Consumer Teleportation, a category that he had invented, they would mention Thorn and the Valley's babies and not his. If they did get mentioned, it would be as an early company that never caught on. It wouldn't matter how big Peared was, how fast it was growing overseas. If Peared was not on the lips of Americans, then it didn't exist.

He could get past that if it wasn't for the second factor, the network effect. Slowly but surely those cooler, more buzzed about companies would start to creep into his markets. It would start with the expats in America. Thirteen percent of the US population was born outside the country. That's forty million people. They set trends for people back home. If expats aren't using Peared, they'll be using its new competitors, Together and Rizon. That means friends and family back home will start using them too. Slowly but surely, he'll lose India, Colombia, the Philippines, and so on. At some point, they'll lose critical mass and then the bottom will fall out. Look at Orkut,

Friendster, and hi5. All gone and replaced by the Valley's baby FriendZone.

There was nowhere on earth he could hide from the libertarian spazzfucks. If they got a toehold, they'd drain him slowly and watch him fade into oblivion. His instincts said make them bleed early and they'll run. While the Valley had all the money in the world, they didn't throw good after bad. If he took Together and Rizon out, the VCs would move on and find an easier market to attack.

They could go privatize zucchini for all he cared; Rabbit just wanted them off his lawn.

Fucking Together. Thorn's startup was really sticking the needle in his eye. First, they hired Frank, then they took their name from his tagline. Bastards. Today, he had heard they were forming the Teleportation Industry Alliance. Over a hundred million people were traveling together with Peared. Did Rabbit get invited as a founding member? Nope, and he shouldn't expect to, either. Ever. At least he knew what he was getting from Thorn. They were going to co-opt him, then crush him.

Frank was kind enough to forward a couple articles this morning. Thorn Capital had announced an $80 million investment in a new teleportation startup called Together. Kleiner, the grandparent of the Valley had led a $120 million round into another one called Rizon. Both were valued at over $500 million and neither had shipped a product yet.

He didn't get it. Do insiders really command that sort of premium? Was Rabbit really that toxic? It was a miscalculation on their part. If they were stupid in that way, then they could be stupid in plenty of other ways.

In the end, he was going to trust his gut.

Kendra and Paolo had drawn up a couple scenarios for owning the US. It was clear they were trying to scare him off the idea, but they were protecting their revenue streams. If he sold to the Valley, they got shit. If he plowed everything overseas into the US, they'd suffer too. For them, the right play was to get as big and rich as possible overseas and then move on once Peared started to stall out. That was the problem with the gunslinger lifestyle. Have gun, will travel, but most of all live to see another day.

Rabbit wasn't in this to see another day. He was in this to show everyone just what he was capable of. It had started all the way back in Menonaqua with his father. That led him to LA, Frank Meyers, and ultimately proving the city of Angels wrong, but now the fucks from up north wanted in on the action.

He'd have to prove them wrong too.

28. BULLETS

The flight in had been noisy. Paolo had barely slept. He'd been up until 2:00 am trying to improve customer acquisition models for South Asia. Pakistan was proving problematic. Now he was sitting in the passenger seat of Sonny's Porsche working on a large coffee. They navigated their way out of LAX, weaving through the courtesy shuttles and Ubers.

"I heard he passed on Thorn Capital," Sonny said.

"What?"

"I have a friend there. He tells me Rabbit turned down $350 million from FriendZone." The car shifted lanes and Sonny made a quick turn off Century up Manchester.

"I'm sorry to hear that," Paolo said. "For you, Em, and the others. An early exit would have been good for you."

"Yes, it would have. My understanding is that it was a bit of a low-ball offer. It sounds like a huge number to me though. It would have paid for my house here, a retirement place for my folks back home, the kids' college and then some. I'm trying to see a bullish glass half full. Should I be seeing things that way, Paolo?"

"If this offer was real, and our projections hold, then yes it was low. I can tell you that much. I'd be worried though."

The car pulled up to a stop light. Sonny turned and looked at Paolo. "Why?"

"He's hell bent on owning America. So far, I can't see a way to do it without playing a very dangerous game."

"Paolo, I know what you do, and I know how you do it. Please be honest with me."

The light changed, Sonny floored the car. A Tesla blew them off the line, but the Porsche ran him down before braking hard at the next light a block away.

"Rabbit wants twenty million users in America before Together and Rizon launch. Em thinks it will cost $10 to get each one, if we can even get that many. Right now, we make $0.12 a month per user. If you run those figures out, it will cost $200 million to get the twenty million he is asking for. We'll be bringing in $108 million in revenue during that time. Our operating margins are forty-five percent. That means we'll have almost $50 million to spend on customer acquisition. Assuming we don't invest in anything else. You see the problem?"

"Yeah, we're $150 million short." Sonny pulled onto La Cienega and accelerated as they drove through Baldwin Hills. Ancient oil derricks pumped up and down as they sped by. Industrial dinosaurs sucking dead dinosaurs from the ground.

"If we had the money, we couldn't spend it that quickly. The entire thing is impossible. The only way to grow that quickly is virally. It's like he thinks I'm some sort of a magician. If we were supposed to have gone viral in the US, we'd have done it by now. People can use the Silicon Valley Code as an excuse, but it's more likely that the US does not want this product. I think this country is too suspicious, too jaded for something like Peared right now. Sure, there are always niche applications, but I look at what he wants to do, and I'm reminded of DraftKings and the other one from college..."

"FanDuel."

"Yes. What a waste of capital. Just like the dockless scooters. Anyways, I've been told we are going to war and my orders are to start stockpiling bullets. Every user is now a way to make bullets and every bullet we make will be fired here, in the US."

"Jesus." They drove down the hill and stopped the light before Jefferson. This used to be nowhere. Now Target had been pushed out and replaced with condos. Transportation corridors can change so much, so fast, even in a city that had sprawled to its borders decades ago.

"Tell me Sonny, are we developing the product at all? Are there ideas to expand it, or change it in some way? I've asked for a product roadmap from Rabbit and it's all about scaling. The product itself is not changing."

"I'm afraid not. It works, we are growing, the orders here are to keep up with growth and let you worry about everything else."

"I'm supposed to worry about everything else? We just discussed what I am worrying about. There's not room in my head for anything else."

The rest of the drive was spent in silence. Each man contemplated his role in completing a nearly impossible task, each man questioning Rabbit's decision making, knowing that Em had already approached him and gotten nowhere on the matter. They were entering into the unknown—not as reckless as sailing off the map, but not as simple as orbiting the dark side of the moon. Somewhere in between lay their darkness and uncertainty. It was time to place their faith in a captain who never listened to his mates.

29. TOEHOLD

Rabbit watched Guy and Girl Sam file into the conference room. The twins with the funny names. They were dressed nearly identically in the uniform of disappointing news. Navy slacks, white starched shirts, open jackets. The only difference between them was in their hair. She went pixie. He was short spiked.

He watched the unconscious coordination between the two. Bags on either side of the conference table. He to the left of the whiteboard, she to the right. They unzipped at the same time. MacBooks out and opened at the same time. She to the projector settings, he to clean the white board off.

Everything Kendra did had a reason to it. Sending them was no different. Their effortless unity was designed to unnerve and suffocate. They ran a game of possession, swallowing up as many opportunities to speak as possible, keeping the client's wrong opinions at bay. Their unconscious twinness passed the baton back and forth between them until a dizzied customer tumbled into their arms.

They were here to tell him that his toehold in America was too small, that it had cost too much to achieve, and that it didn't have a pathway forward. The first half of their presentation was an overview of spend and performance. Big numbers out, tiny trickles in. The second half would show deterioration overseas. They'd lean in, emphasizing that Peared was slowing, and that bullet production was killing the business.

He didn't need the Sams to tell him he'd wasted $20 million

dollars, and he wasn't about to let them run their parlor trick on him.

Rabbit could change tactics with the best of them. Now he needed to see if these two weirdos were amongst the best, or if they were just here to deliver a message. He walked into the conference room, unplugged the projector, and then sat down at the far end of the table.

"I saw the presentation. I don't need it spoon fed to me."

"You could have cancelled or setup a call then. We flew down for this," Girl Sam said.

"No, you flew down for this. I want to know how to salvage that $20 million I just spent."

"The numbers are the numbers," Guy Sam said.

"But the perception is something different. If I can't win America, then I want to make sure no one wins America. I want to poison the pool," Rabbit replied.

"Interesting."

Girl Sam looked over at Guy. Rabbit got up and poured waters for everyone. He had changed the gravity in the room. Better to give them a moment to recalibrate. He didn't know how the twin telepathy worked, but there was no reason to rush now.

"What's the ultimate goal?" they asked.

"I win. The others shutdown."

"That's fairly broad," Guy said.

"It's very concrete. I want them to think America is the market to own. I want them to ignore everywhere else. I want to make America unwinnable. By the time they realize the mistake, it will be too late."

At this point he watched the Sams detach. Guy Sam grabbed a pen and paper and Girl Sam took over the conversation.

"We are two months from the launch of Together and Rizon. You've invested $20 million in this market and got 500k customers out of it. Outside the US, Peared signs up almost a million people a day and doesn't spend a dime. The first thing we need to do is talk up the importance of America without breaking out any stats on America. Just throw the overall tonnage of the business at people. It will take a couple months for them to figure out the US is not where it's at," she said.

"Right—we bluff. People think we have a $20 million stack in front of us," Rabbit said, drumming his hands on the conference room table.

"Where we go from there is tricky. You can't keep spending at that level, but you need to be spending here. Em needs to make it look like you are still in the US even if you aren't. We can't just go silent. That calls for stupid spend. Billboards, celebrity endorsers, anything but the online stuff that costs a lot of money."

"Billboards. Put Lebron on them."

"Something like that. You'd be surprised how cheap they are nowadays. Billboards, not Lebron. He'll cost you a pretty penny. We'll need someone else."

"Ok, maybe someone who is big here, but much bigger overseas. Two birds, one stone," Rabbit said.

"Yes, that's good thinking. Now we need a trap."

"Scare the shit out of people. Fake kidnap someone on Rizon. No—do it on Together."

"Easy Rabbit. That's going nuclear on the pool, not poisoning it. You can turn those services into cesspools without kidnapping anyone. You remember Chat Roulette?"

"The dick site?"

"Exactly. Both Together and Rizon are going to have very small numbers of users early on. It's going to cost a lot of money to acquire them. Now if one in every three of them ends up with a set of Eyes that ask the Hands to whip their dicks out they are going to have a major quality of service problem. Now they are in a Catch 22 situation. Can't spend more in marketing until you clean up the cesspool, can't clean up the cesspool until you get better users."

Rabbit smiled.

"I need to sell my bullets and start buying trolls."

"Exactly."

Guy Sam slid the piece of paper across the table to his sister. She looked down and studied it for a moment. Her fingernail went to one item. A silent question passed across. He nodded in affirmation.

"We think you can poison America for $5 million a month and that it will take six months to ruin the market. The more trolls you add, the higher your competitor's acquisition cost, the faster they burn through their money. Our guess is that it will cost you $30 million give or take $5 million to kill Together and Rizon."

"I can afford that."

"We know you can and it's well within our acceptable tolerance levels. We'll report back to Kendra. She'll be happy with your change in tactics."

"Tell Kendra you are joining the Peared team until Together and Rizon are out of business. I need someone sophisticated to do this, and Paolo has to drive the rest of the world. Tell Kendra it's not a request. It's the soundest investment she can make."

30. CASINGS

Paolo had no idea where he was, other than the floor. Next to him was a woman wearing a white tank top covered in dark red splotches. She had no bottoms on. He felt a surge of adrenaline and panic fired all his synapses at once. He jerked up. He was naked. Deep scratch marks ran down his chest. She had drawn blood. His clothes were all over the floor. Everything was on the floor—empty bottles, half smoked joints, a coke-dusted mirror. He turned and looked at her. Her smeared raccoon eyes contrasted hard against her shallow yellow skin. There were bruises up and down her arms. A choke collar was tight around her neck.

Next to her were two pairs of AR glasses.

What had he gotten himself into?

He looked to the left. They were at the side of a perfectly good bed. He pulled himself up and crawled into it, pulling the white down comforter over his head. The dark felt better. He peeked out from it and looked at the woman. From this vantage he could see her chest rising up and down as she inhaled then exhaled. She was alive. That was good. He pulled the covers over his head. It took a moment to place the smell, but he realized why they were on the floor. The bed stank of piss.

He got out of the bed and kneeled over her. The splotches were red wine. They had spilled quite a bit. Not spilled, thrown. Splatter marks were all over the walls and the heavy carpet. He picked up a wine glass and put it on the table. He looked back over the woman. He had no recollection of her. A vein in her neck throbbed just above the collar. He leaned down, unfastened the choker, and slipped the leather from around her neck. Paolo placed it on the table next to the glass. Her neck was red and tender. That was going to turn into a nasty mark.

He felt a familiar searing sensation. Instinctively he looked at his palms. There were past marks from climbing incidents, but nothing fresh. No, it was his wrists. They had been bound. He looked back at the bed and saw the ropes hanging from the headboard. He had a dim memory of her shoveling coke up his nose. She wouldn't untie him, then something weird happened. He couldn't remember what, but he laughed so hard he pissed the bed. That's where it got ugly. She smacked him hard enough to see stars.

He stepped around a couple used condoms. At least that wasn't a worry.

Paolo found the shower. He turned the heat up, let the steam build, and sat on the smooth stone ground. The horrors of the night evaporated off his skin and lifted up into the steam. He could smell booze and the sick sweat of amphetamines. Smoke too. He started to throw up. On his hands and knees, convulsions, the remnants of the night disappearing down the drain. Water running down his face. Over his back.

What had he gotten himself into?

The night had started with dinner. Kendra, Rabbit, and Malcolm DuBour. Mastro's Ocean Club in Malibu. It was a simple meet and greet. He had the surf and turf. At some point Rabbit left for a date. They drove down to the marina. Malcolm wanted to take them out on his Sunseeker. That woman was on the boat. She served him a white Bordeaux. He didn't remember a damn thing after that.

He toweled off and found a bathrobe. It was white and fluffy like a bunny. He wandered downstairs and across the great room until he found the kitchen. He walked in. Kendra was sitting there. Her eyes were bloodshot, but otherwise she looked ok.

She got up from her chair, walked over to Paolo and smacked him hard across the face. She got him in the same spot as last night. It stung wickedly.

"That was for some of the things you did to me."

Then she gave him a hug and whispered in his ear. "I hope you'll forgive me for what I did to you."

"What did you do to me?"

"I was the Eyes. She was the Hands."

"Kendra. What the fuck?"

"Malcolm was your Eyes. You were his Hands. Get dressed. Let's get out of here. I don't want to say anything else while we are in this place."

31. THE CROSS

The car pulled up to a red light. They had not spoken since the kitchen. Kendra broke the silence.

"We are going into the centaur business. Last night was your price of admission."

Paolo turned and looked at her. His eyes bulging, nostrils flared.

"Come again?"

"You remember that call from Vegas? When I asked, you had it all figured out right then and there. Like it was meant to be. We are going to develop and manage the centaur crowd coordination process. Malcolm is going to funnel jobs our way and arrange for local support on operations."

"What does that have to do with you drugging me?"

"Last night is all on tape. I have a copy. He has a copy. She has a copy. You'll get a copy. With that tape, any one of us will have the ability to ruin the rest of us. It's an insurance policy that secures our enterprise."

"Kendra, I don't want to do centaurs. It's dirty work that crosses the line."

"I know you don't. Now you know why I drugged you."

"What's on that tape?"

"Enough to kill your green card."

The light turned, and her black Audi resumed its course

down Pico. Paolo stared out the window at the passing apartments, coffee shops, and 7-11s. Fresh blood stains leaked through his t-shirt.

"Jesus fucking Christ. I've known you a long, long time Kendra. What you did to me last night crossed a big line. What is going on with you? Why do you think that knocking me out and sexually assaulting me is worth my green card?"

She ignored his question.

"We have a window with Peared to make fuck you money. I thought that was going to be through Rabbit. Now he's got the Valley after him. He is making maneuvers which while right, are expensive and uncertain. I want a return on investment, and centaurs are the answer."

"I asked you a question."

"It's not a question you can afford. Sorry, not sorry."

"Fuck off Kendra."

"We are doing this without Rabbit. This is you, me, Malcolm, and his assistant. Rabbit is not reliable enough for this level of risk."

"Cunt."

She waited him out. The Audi continued down the block in silence. Kendra held all the cards. She knew that Paolo's life was in the US, that Chile was a million years away. While it was a stretch to call Paolo a true adult, he was a child when he left his homeland. Going back now wasn't an option.

She thought it would take longer than it did, at the next light Paolo spoke.

"You don't have a problem driving mobs to beat the shit out of people?"

"No."

"I do."

"I know, which is why I needed leverage on you. This is a dirty business Paolo, but I've done worse. Hell, you've done worse. You just think that breaking minds and emotions is not as bad as breaking bones. Let me tell you, it is."

"Which part of me did you break last night?"

Kendra didn't answer that, but Paolo knew it wasn't a part of him, it was him. Somewhere in the middle of their conversation, his mind had already started working on the centaur problem. It was spinning up that murky place in his brain which endlessly slaved away on the hard problems. One afternoon it would serve the answer up as a neatly solved epiphany, and then it would be time to get to work building the solution.

He wouldn't know how he really felt about this turn of events until he watched the end product in action. He might not feel a thing. Maybe Kendra knew that already.

32. BACK OFFICES

It had sounded so easy when first whispered over third martinis. It had felt so close to her the night she turned Paolo. Now Kendra was faced with the reality of making it happen. She looked at the top right corner of her whiteboard. The word CentOps, short for Centaur Operations Center, was written in red. No one but her knew what it meant. She kept it there as a constant reminder that it was the fastest way to make money off Peared.

Malcolm had offered to staff and build it, but she didn't want to give him all the power. Once it was set up and running, there'd be nothing to keep him from pushing her out. He was the source of their jobs, so he'd be able to take 100% of everything. Despite not knowing anyone in the paramilitary world, she insisted they handle the process, the connection into Peared, and the command staff to manage their mobs. The reality was that Paolo was the only person who could tap into the Peared network and design the process. Even if she trusted Malcolm, she couldn't leave that delicate act of manipulation to him. He was a brute-force, most-direct-route, sort of guy. That had its appeal, but for this she needed a patient and persevering maestro. She needed a man with invisible fingers.

Kendra had shipped Paolo out to Abu Dhabi for a private security convention. They needed to start somewhere. Paolo could talk automation and intrusion detection with the best of them. She wasn't sure how he was going to bridge that into recruiting mercenaries.

Thinking a little more, she realized he had no business being there. She opened Telegram and shot him a message.

"Head home tonight. Need to rethink."

"Tonight?"

"Yes. I can get you on Emirates to JFK."

"Why the change?"

"Will explain later."

"I'd rather fly direct to SFO."

"It's sold out. Would like you out of there ASAP."

"Fine."

Kendra closed the app and paced the room slowly. This needed to be done differently. She needed disposable people, not specialists. If anything went wrong, it had to lead to a dead end, not to a room full of paramilitary. She needed fast, cheap, and out of control.

Kendra wiped CentOps off her whiteboard. She replaced it with Engineered Chaos. She didn't know what that meant just yet, but it would come to her.

33. LONG HAUL

He considered clearing customs at JFK and catching a car to Astoria. He had spent six weeks there visiting his cousin during the 2014 World Cup. The bars were packed with Colombianas in tight yellow shirts and Brazilian girls in hip huggers. Every team had supporters driving up Steinway, hands on their horns, flags out the windows. Chile had nearly upset Brazil on PKs. Paolo slept on the couch every night and never complained. Now he was flying first class on Emirates and annoyed at the way the seat reclined.

He let his daydream die. The bars would still be there, but he'd never be able to go back. That window was closed.

The buzz of steady drink service and binge watching was wearing off. His mind turned to Kendra. She had called him back after two days in Abu Dhabi. Her indecision sentenced him to twenty-four hours of travel time. Changing her mind was very unlike her and it made him nervous. First, she drugged and blackmailed him, then she sent him halfway around the world on a fool's errand. That was not a stable operating pattern.

Paolo took a moment to check in with himself. He looked at the time on his watch. He bit his gum. He looked around the cabin for anything very out of place. All was normal. As a kid he had spent a month using those three tricks to try to catch himself in a dream. Lucidity never came to him.

After the drugged night, he had picked those tricks back up. This time to make sure he was in control of himself.

Fool me twice, shame on me, he thought.

The tape had been shocking to watch. Not for the outrageousness or the sexual violence, but because it triggered no additional memories. Nothing came to him other than what he had recalled in the shower. He watched himself and the woman spend six hours turning that room into a disaster area, and nothing came to him except for those few flashes. It made him nervous to lose that much time. Even worse, Kendra was right—that tape would sink his green card. Multiple drug offenses.

He considered finding the woman from that night. Was his dance partner in depravity complicit or clueless like him? Did it matter? He wasn't sure, but he wanted to talk. While Paolo could compartmentalize with the best of them, there was one piece of cognitive dissonance he couldn't bury.

He wanted to do it again.

He had spent the week since it happened trying to deny the thought, but a part of him kept bringing it to the surface. *Do it again,* it cried out.

Maybe that's what Kendra was banking on.

A chill came over him and he shuddered. He pressed the attendant button. She approached with a scotch in hand. Paolo realized he was the drink button guy in first class. Not a good look. He asked for a water to save face, but took the scotch. The warmth seeped into his gums, rubbing itself over the rawness caused from the hourly biting. He swallowed and felt his buzz returning. Two more hours to NYC, a three-hour layover, and then another six to San Francisco. While he was happy to be flying up front, he would have preferred the shorter route going direct.

He hadn't slept a wink the entire flight. He'd take something at the terminal to make sure he slept during the next leg. There would be no rest for him at NAM.

34. TROLLS R' US

It was Sonny's third visit to Tijuana. He stared out the window, watching the city center fade to low slung warehouses and small factories. The silver Chevy Tahoe pulled off the main drag into an industrial park. The last time he'd come here, it had been to see 80,000 square feet of nothingness. He had feigned interest in the barebones facility, but inspecting internet connections and redundant power did nothing for him.

Actually, it had made him wonder what he was doing with his career.

Sonny had been tasked with managing the troll operation. It was his own fault really. Had he not asked into the inner circle, he'd have never known it existed. Now he was in charge of it. Sonny was a man of process and documentation, consensus and collaboration. He should be in the middle of company HQ making sure objectives were aligned, and teams were on target. He didn't like being out on an island, and he didn't like being in charge of something secret. Despite his earlier pledge, he hadn't told Em or Paolo what he was up to. Paolo likely knew—he knew everything it seemed—but Em wouldn't go in for this. Not one bit. It was a black-ops designed to knock out a competitor. Sonny didn't have the time to build out the facility and referee a fight between Rabbit and her. He chose the path of least resistance.

The lights went on. Before him were countless cubes, organized in neat rows that stretched to the back of the building. Their new partner, Omar Gomez, extended his arms with pride.

"All of this in the last two weeks. I told you we'd hit our targets."

Omar slapped Sonny on the back. He cringed from the unwanted contact. His host was a short, excitable man with thin black hair. He was wearing a starched white dress shirt tucked into beat up jeans which tucked into fancy cowboy boots. A large silver belt buckle held everything together.

Sonny was impressed. He had managed a few office build outs and knew that progress like this required around-the-clock work. Nights and weekends. Extra guys and hurry-up deliveries.

"How is hiring coming?"

"We've filled one hundred seats. They start training next week. We'll hire in batches of fifty after that. Bring on a new group every other week. We can move faster if you need it. I'd love to fill this as quick as I can. I'm after corporate clients, real work, like sales and customer service, but I need to show hundreds of bodies already at work to land them. That's were Peared comes in. You help me fill the gap."

"You know what we discussed. We'll fill as many seats as make sense. No promises beyond 200 for three months."

"Of course."

Sonny had not expected to end up in Tijuana. When he was first given the assignment, he assumed he'd go to the usual suspects in Manila or Bangladesh. First, they'd be cheaper. Second, they'd be farther away and easier to hide. The problem was effectiveness. He had gone to Asia and met with several centers that specialized in "community participation," the industry euphemism for this sort of work. Things looked good until they tested agents against Peared users in America. Something didn't click. After a few weeks of trials, Sonny realized that US users wouldn't give them the time of day. There was a cultural barrier and impatience that caused them to bail right away.

Omar understood this. He knew that Americans liked to feel big and nothing was worse than making them feel small. To effectively troll one didn't need to gross out, they needed to embarrass. His plan was to only hire people who had been in the US, who understood how all the little things worked and how people talked. They weren't going to ask people to whip their dicks out, they were going to take their Hands into Starbucks, screw up the order over and over while the line backed up, and then give their name as Mr. Shitzenpants. Mortification was their weapon.

The best part? If anyone discovered the center and asked who hired them, Omar would claim no one. He'd say it was a new center with idle seats who weren't being properly overseen. He'd blame a non-existent manager and say it was all a cruel game some rogue employees were playing to kill the time.

It worked for Sonny.

What didn't work for Sonny was where this was all going. Together and Rizon raised $200 million between them. They were backed by the two most important VCs in the valley. Rabbit's plan was to ruin the customer experience, so they went out of business. If he won, it would be by making the space toxic. That would make Peared toxic as well. While Rabbit would have the satisfaction of being right, Sonny's options were worthless unless someone bought the company.

Who was going to buy Peared after Thorn and Kleiner walked away from the space?

He had negotiated an $80k bump in salary for taking the troll job on, but success would likely close out any chance of an acquisition. Had Rabbit accepted Thorn's $350 million offer to sell, Sonny would have made $3.5 million. Massive difference.

He needed to talk to Rabbit and find out his plans after he beat Rizon and Together. Was there something beyond that or was ego everything to Rabbit?

Sonny had to know whether he was working for a genius or a fool.

35. DOG AND PONY SHOWS

Rabbit watched as a single white male in his mid-twenties walked to the center of the stage. A spotlight beamed down on him, illuminating his smart denim jeans, black mock turtleneck, and trademark Birkenstocks. His name was Elliot Blank, and he was the little shit that Thorn had given $80 million. Rabbit stared at the screen, sizing up his new mortal enemy.

Behind Elliot, a light purple screen projected the word Together in bright white letters.

"We are here today to talk about an amazing transformation in human communication. For ages we've imagined the ability to put ourselves in another place. The ancients called it astral projection; science fiction called it teleportation. This ability has been out of reach until now. Ladies and gentlemen, I present Together." Elliot motioned to the screen and a video began to play.

Rabbit watched the slickly produced video introduce a carbon copy of Peared. The interface was a little cleaner, the graphics slightly better, but the same functionality and commands were all there. They had ripped Peared off verbatim. The voiceover talked about Hands and Eyes, and the collective Consciousness between Pairs. The match process, the signaling, even the little glamours were all there. It was his fucking product wearing someone else's clothes. Rabbit gripped his tumbler, fingertips pressed white against the glass, taut knuckles a mix of yellow and red. He picked it off his desk and hurled the glass at his office window. Instead of shattering, it bounced back, nearly hitting him.

"The balls on these people," Rabbit said to himself.

He pulled his phone out and shot an angry text to Frank Meyers. "You no-pride thieving hack piece of shit. Enjoy today. It will be Together's last good one."

Thirty minutes later in a theater across the street, Rizon made its debut.

"I'd like to say that we were the very first people to introduce teleportation, but Together booked their theater quicker than us. That's okay, because here at Rizon, we don't aim to be first, we aim to be best. Having our competition introduce their product the same day as us creates a healthy rivalry. It pushes us to be better. Most of all, it shows that the Valley is still the world's center of innovation."

He'd never made two mortal enemies in one day, but there was a first time for everything. Albie Hammel was definitely his new mortal enemy. Another single white guy in his mid-twenties on stage and stealing his idea. This one was wearing a $700 hoodie and a pair of khakis. He had $120 million of Kleiner's money and a clone of Rabbit's fucking product. Where Elliot was clearly aping Steve Jobs right down to the wireframe glasses, Albie was cut from the bro fork of the startup tree. He stood six and a half feet tall, blonde-haired and blue-eyed, and clearly a fan of the gym. Rabbit immediately sized him up as a leader and not a doer. He could synthesize and inspire, but he doubted Albie ever had an original thought.

The demo clearly showed that. It was Peared all over again, just a little more aggro and gamer-centric. At least they had put some of their own personality into the branding instead of Together's basic bitch minimalism. Rabbit clicked off halfway through their presentation. He had seen enough and knew what was coming next.

While the media would pitch the dual launch as an amazing coincidence for a budding rivalry, Rabbit was far more cynical. He knew that they had planned it all out. How else would they book theaters opposite each other and plan launch events an hour apart? It was clearly staged so that the lapdogs in the tech media could go from one event to another, load up on their speaking points, and spout out the canned bullshit the VCs wanted spread. Expect profile pieces comparing and contrasting the founders. Expect a manufactured rivalry to get breathless coverage. Expect them to never ever mention Peared as the basis for the entire space.

It was all a giant fucking whitewashing. A conspiracy of backscratchers to wipe Rabbit off the face of the earth.

He had seen this coming and was having none of it. Let them spend their money on fancy launch parties. Let them sponsor the Golden State Warriors. Let them read their own clippings until their shit stops stinking. Rabbit would be waiting for them where it mattered. He was going to cut them to bits. He was going to bleed millions from the masters of the universe. He was going to bleed them until there wasn't another drop left. After that Elliot and Albie could take a year off, write up blog posts about the important lessons they learned, and move on to the next thing.

While they did that, Rabbit would go to bed every night with a single thought in his head. Satisfaction was his.

36. PUSHER MAN

Paolo had been working the problem since he touched down at SFO.

How do you find people who want to watch the world burn? How do you get them to flame one target and not another? How do you keep wildfire from spreading out of control?

He wasn't sure it could be done.

The first part was easy. Peared was filled with sociopaths. Some of his earliest work was identifying them and keeping them isolated from the general population. They were called Evil Eyes around the office. Generally, they cycled through accounts, but used the same VR headset. You could find them from their low ratings and short connection times. They'd pair up and drop people over and over until they found someone willing to do their bidding.

Until now, there was no need to do anything other than quarantine them.

Now the task was to find people who wanted the same bad outcomes, pair them with people who followed orders, and push them all down the same road to hell. Kendra's orders. She didn't think you needed controllers coordinating multiple Hands. She thought all you needed was enough powder and a match. They were inciting chaos, not performing surgery. Give humans the right conditions, and they'd do the rest. Besides, clients would be willing to accept collateral damage if they got the outcome they wanted.

It sounded simple coming from her lips, but the challenge was to do it invisibly. Paolo preferred more elegant solutions, but this approach had the lowest likelihood of being detected. Privatize the benefit and socialize the risk.

He decided to start simply and work his way out.

Right now, he was following the Phish comeback tour around the US. Today, they were up at Watkins Glen. In the middle of their show they did a cover band bit and played audience requests. It was a perfect testing ground for Paolo. After five shows he was able to identify people attending the show with AR glasses and match them to Peared users at home. Now, he was trying to get the Pairs to all want the same cover song.

The band was in a frenzied jam. After this they would take requests. He pushed the melody to Over the Rainbow to his test group. No one could hear it over Trey Anastasio's guitar, but it was there working its way into their heads. Their brains would pick it up and process it as a memory from earlier, one of those unplaceable earworms. As the decibels increased from the stage, he pushed the volume up and quickly flashed glamour effects, ruby red slippers, falling barns, and yellow brick roads, across their glasses. Hopefully some of them would be tripping or take it as a flashback. He needed them to translate those quick glamours as a sign the band should play that song.

The jam ended in a crash of cymbals and Phish took a moment to catch their breath. Paolo waited, watching twenty views of the band across five split monitors. The aging rockers slurped down water from cheap plastic bottles. Finally, they asked the audience for requests. Paolo hit the record button. He'd have to parse out the responses of forty different people, twenty Eyes and twenty Hands. That wasn't nearly enough to cut through the crowd of 20,000, but he wasn't trying to influence the stage yet. He was trying to get his little ants in the crowd to pick the same song out of a million possibilities.

If he could do that, he was well on his way. Herding hippies was far harder than swaying undecideds into a simple choice of yes or no, cheer or boo. Their centaur jobs would involve getting a crowd to make a binary decision.

Once he could do that, it was just a matter of amplification and intensity.

He heard the classic riff to Layla kick in. He turned his recordings off and dropped out of God Mode. It was time to analyze the streams and see how much further he had to go.

37. AFTERWORD

Sonny walked into Rabbit's office and shut the door behind him. He wanted to have this conversation yesterday, then he saw Rabbit fling a glass tumbler off his window. Rabbit was staring at a printout of the balance sheet. He looked briefly at his COO, waved him into a seat, and went back to the numbers. Sonny waited for an opening. None was coming.

His buzzing phone broke the silence. Omar was looking for the green light to go live. Sonny quizzed him over Telegram then gave the thumbs up. He put his phone away and looked across the desk; Rabbit was still deep in finances.

"Is now not a good time?" Sonny asked.

"Now is a fine time. I've been waiting for you to say something."

Sonny looked at him—his eyes were down on the sheet. He hated Rabbit's ability to read and have a conversation at the same time. While Rabbit found it efficient, Sonny found it dismissive. Especially for the topic at hand.

"I wanted to update you on our center in Tijuana."

"Go ahead, update."

"Well, everything is ready. We have one hundred seats online now. Another fifty are about to complete training and will begin on Thursday. I've walked through the rules of engagement with Omar and reviewed the roleplaying sessions the center did with agents. I feel good about their preparation and gave Omar the green light to go live."

"Excellent. Well done Kumar."

"Rabbit, can I get your attention for a minute?"

"You have it."

"I'm sorry, but I need your eyes on me. I can't talk to you like this."

Rabbit looked up at him. "Fine. What is so important?"

"When I took this task, we discussed what it would likely do to Peared's standing in the US and our prospects for acquisition. We had a frank and candid conversation and came to an agreement that it would likely close the door for a quick acquisition of the business."

"You're not shaking me down again."

Sonny shook his head. "No, I am not. However, I am looking for some clarity on what comes afterwards."

"Afterwards?"

"Yes. Assuming that we achieve our objective and shutter Together and Rizon, there's the question of what comes next."

Rabbit put his paperwork on the desk and chuckled. "And you want to know what comes next?"

"Yes."

"Okay Sonny, here's the thing. We are getting up on the wire. Do you know what I am talking about?"

"No."

"The high wire. We are stepping up there right now. It's a dangerous place with little margin for error. The only people who should go there are the people equipped to handle it. When you are up on the wire, your only focus is the task at hand. You don't worry about getting groceries later or whether that girl you're fucking wants a relationship. Those things cloud your judgement. They cost you the edge needed to do the job. So, when I am up on the wire, I don't think about anything else. My vision becomes singular and focused."

Sonny looked at him, trying to decide what to say next. "That's understandable, but I imagine that before you get on the wire you have some idea of what happens once you get off of it."

"Sonny, a skilled operator, someone really good like myself, knows that it's important to always leave outs. The future is not a straight path, it's a branching tree. At every fork you need to be able to read and react. People who get hung up on final destinations get disappointed. People who view it as a journey make the most of the opportunities that present themselves."

Jesus Christ, he's making it up as he goes along, Sonny thought.

"Rabbit, you're a hypocrite. You have a final destination, and it's King of California. The thing is, Peared doesn't end when you get crowned the winner. It goes on, but no one here knows in what shape or form. Are you going to sell? Will you run it forever? What's in it for us when you win? You turned down $350 million a couple months ago. $35 million of that would have gone into the employee option pool."

"You get a nice fat check twice a month, but that's not enough huh?"

"I could get that same check from a dozen places in town."

"Then why are you here?" Rabbit shot back.

"I'm here for the exit. You remember when you said you were going to make Peared a monster?"

"Of course."

"I assumed that meant the next Google or FriendZone."

"So, you thought there was a pot of gold waiting for you?"

"You know how this game gets played Rabbit. Paychecks are one thing but cashing out is how all us little people get crowned. Where does Peared go after it ruins the American market and puts its competitors out of business?"

"It goes wherever it wants to."

Sonny threw his hands up. "There you are with generalities again."

"If you want someone to tell you they're going to make you a millionaire, dust off your resume and start making calls. You are a very talented person. I'm sure plenty of people will whisper sweet nothings in your ear and sell you the fantasy you want to hear. What I'm telling you is that we can't think about a future until we ruin Together and Rizon. If you demand certainty, then get the fuck out of my building."

38. OMAR'S ARMY

Rabbit stood behind the one-way mirror and looked out at the sea of cubicles. The first third was filled with agents. They had their VR glasses on, trolling away. Beside Rabbit, the Sams were looking at a dashboard that monitored and aggregated everything taking place on the floor.

"Ok, are you ready to watch the team in action?" Omar asked.

"Let's see what you got." Rabbit rubbed his hands together.

Omar turned on a bank of monitors. He rigged it to see into any agent's VR stream and watch their Pair in action. He brought a session onto the big monitor.

"What are we doing?" a woman asked.

"We are going to the subway to beg for money," Agent Vargas replied.

"Why?"

"Because I'm poor and I need to practice panhandling. How can I get better if I can't practice? Now let's head over to that dumpster. We need to find a cardboard box to make a sign with."

The screen went black as the woman dropped the call. Omar selected another from the queue.

"Stand-up?" a man asked.

"Yes, it's open mic night. I've got some new jokes that I want to test out," Agent Cameron replied.

"You're a comedian?"

"Well, sort of. I'm actually an oncologist, but at night I like to do comedy. These new jokes are going to kill. You like dad jokes, right?"

"Can you tell me one?"

"Not until you are up onstage. I want it to be fresh for you when you deliver the line."

It went black again. A moment later Omar switched to another agent.

"Here's the CVS. What happens next?" a woman asked.

"So, here's the thing. Last week I slept with a guy I shouldn't have. We live in a small town where everybody knows everyone, including the pharmacist. Now I'm worried that this guy might have given me the clap, but I can't go to my drugstore because then it will get back to my mom and well, he's her ex-boyfriend. So, I need you to go and describe my symptoms to them and get a diagnosis." Agent Diaz answered.

Rabbit chortled as the screen went black and another came online.

"You what?" a man asked.

"I can't go to lunch with a woman who is not my wife. It's against my beliefs. The thing is, she's done a lot of really great work at the office and it's her last day on the job. So, I need you to take her to lunch as me." Agent Hernandez answered.

"This is too weird."

Omar hit the mute button and turned to Rabbit, a huge smile across his face.

"What do you think?" Omar asked Rabbit.

"I think it's a fucking riot. How many of these are you doing?"

"Each rep averages 4.7 Pairs an hour. On any given day, we've got 120 seats full and they are logged in for seven hours, so we do about 4000 pairs a day. We measure them on drop rate after one minute. To be successful, an agent needs to get 80% of their Pairs to go for at least one minute and then have the other party drop the session."

"What happens if the other side doesn't hang up?"

"We give them ten minutes, then if it's still going, our reps start getting weirder and more annoying. If someone won't hang up after fifteen minutes, we assume they are fucking with us and we drop the session."

"How often does that happen?" Rabbit asked.

"We get maybe a hundred a day. Our people are very good at being awkward."

"Any difference between Together and Rizon?"

"Together users are easier to scare off. It's more mainstream, they have fewer defenses. The Rizon guys are used to trash talking and people saying weird shit from video games. We get less of them, but they are a tougher crowd. I think we'll need to switch our tactics with them. I've got some of our bros cooking up a playbook."

"Good. I want to take Together down first. You keep hammering them, Omar."

They left the facility and began the drive back into town. The Sams sat together in the backseat, a laptop resting between them.

"Looks like Sonny and Omar did a good job," Rabbit said.

"By appearances, yes," Guy Sam said.

"What's your assessment?" Rabbit asked, his eyes darting up at the rearview mirror.

"Too soon to tell. Our program will take in stats from Omar's agents. It also crawls the profile pages on both sites and checks the last login date for every Together and Rizon user. We'll use that to develop an abandonment rate. Once that's in place, all we need to do is compare and contrast churn rates. We look at people who have paired with someone in Omar's Army vs. those who haven't. The expectation is that talking to an Omar agent will lead to a much higher churn rate. If churn is the same and the agents are not scaring people off, then we'll need to abandon the program. If they are successful, then we need to do some forecasting," Girl Sam said.

"To see if we can pull this off," Rabbit said.

"Right. It's one thing to be able to scare users away. It's another to create a bad enough reputation that the service fails. Getting from the former to the latter is a matter of figuring out the key variables. How fast does Together grow? How much money do they spend to get those users? How cheaply can we run them off the site?"

"Well, I've got you two to figure out the quantitative. Qualitatively though, that shit was a riot. I told Omar to start posting the best ones on YouTube."

"Yes, they are very amusing," Guy Sam said.

Rabbit looked in his rearview and watched the two of them go back to the laptop. He regretted not taking Omar up on his offer of dinner and drinks. Next trip he'd leave the square twins at home and plan on having a good time. Despite the downers in back, he felt great about this decision. His gut had told him to own America. He had failed there, but it led him to a plan for stopping his rivals. That was life up on the wire.

39. WE'RE ONLY SCIENCE

Paolo laid down on the sofa and traveled back in time. Before he discovered climbing, psychology, and computers, Paolo had been a lost teen. He was the kid that was too smart for his high school and too wild for his family. Earning a full scholarship to USC had been a godsend. He enrolled early and was out of his house as soon as possible.

His first purchase had been a used Honda motorcycle. It opened the dark streets and infinite highways of Los Angeles. He prowled up and down those Hollywood nights in search of kindred spirits, finding them in places like the Parlour Club and Death, Death, Disco.

That was a lifetime ago, as unreachable now as his summer in Astoria. The rigors of his program and a desire to make a career in the US brought him into the daylight. By grad school he started getting up at times he used to go to bed at. Still, the music remained. Dark wave, 80s synths, electroclash. He watched the late summer sunset fade and the lights of Los Gatos come up. He missed LA. Nothing was ever boring there.

Paolo reached for his phone and dialed Kendra.

"Paolo?"

"You said to call sometime. You know, just to say hi."

"Hi."

"Did I catch you at a bad time?" he asked, turning down his speaker.

"Not at all. You're feeling something aren't you?"

"I am."

Paolo had spent the last hour wandering around his condo, unable to focus, debating the wisdom of making this call. Kendra had been slow-playing him all this time. For months she had drip-fed him doses of attraction. Each flirtation small enough to not cross a line, but still so potent to a digital man-child, deprived of release, consumed by work. Then that night happened. She knocked him cold, mainlined his desires, and left him with only the memory of how good it felt to be bad. That night, she showed Paolo more, showed him what it could feel like when you no longer gave a fuck. Peared was so much better when you played outside the lines. When you took the job, the people, and the power and pushed past all the boundaries.

"Want to tell me about it?" Kendra asked.

He hesitated, knowing she was miles ahead of him. Paolo had come to realize that her threat of blackmail wasn't a threat. She was giving him an easy justification for the wrong she wanted. That night was wiring his chemical and emotional pathways. The following morning was laying the moral groundwork for doing it again. Carrot and stick wrapped up in sex, drugs, and tech. A green card played on the table.

Knowing his buttons were being pushed, that he was being manipulated, amplified the temptation. She was appealing to the operator in him. This was the game she said. *Bad* is the optimal play, and this is how fucking good it feels.

"I'm not sure."

"That's fine. Tell me about your weekend. Any plans?"

"I'm going climbing on Saturday, getting up early, back late. On Sunday I'm heading to a family friend's place for dinner."

"What else are you doing on Sunday?"

"Nothing. It's an all-day meal. She's a chef from Santiago. Looks after some of us when we need home cooking."

"Seems like a waste of a day."

He could hear the dismissiveness in her voice. How dull the basic comfort of home cooking was when this dark tangled thing was right there waiting for him.

"She going to set you up with someone?" The implication that a meal wasn't enough.

"She's run out of girls to try with."

"Someone's picky or just afraid to take a chance?"

"I just don't want other people making those sorts of decisions for me. Besides, I'm still young. Not ready to settle down."

"Paolo, you're thirty-two. I was your resident advisor your freshman year. Sometimes you just need to get on a train when it pulls into the station."

"I know."

"So, you ready to tell me about it?"

Paolo swallowed. Fuck it. He was going to jump in.

"I want to do it again. With her, and you."

"Paolo."

"Let's not play games Kendra. That's what that video was for."

"So, you liked it?"

"I don't remember any of it."

"And that's what you liked, isn't it?"

"Yes." Paolo felt a rush as he vocalized the thought for the first time. Not remembering a damn thing was the perfect high for a man who knew too much.

"I shouldn't tell you this."

"What?"

"I want to do it again too."

"God, Kendra. This is fucked up."

"I know, and I love it."

"Why can't we be normal?"

"Because this is so much better, Paolo."

"Does it have to be with Malcolm?"

"If you want her, you get him. Besides, I want him running you. Something clicked with us that night. It's never been so good."

"You'd done this before?"

"Of course, darling. I'd have never done that to my precious Paolo without knowing he'd be ok."

"Kendra, who's driving this, you or Malcolm?"

"Maybe it's mutual. Does it matter?"

"I suppose not. So, when can we do it again?"

"Not until we do a job first. How far along are you?"

And there it was. The cost of the ticket to take the ride.

"I'm getting there."

"What does that mean?"

He felt her flipping him again, right back to work and the task of making her rich.

"I can put all the people together and most of the time I can get them to do what I want. The final piece is constructing missions that the system never registers. I need to spin up multiple missions that link the Pairs together."

"That's real progress. How hard is the last part?"

"I know how to do it, just not sure if I'm capable of programming it. If I can't I'll find a work around."

"Keep pushing. Malcolm tells me there's something in six weeks if you are ready."

"I'll let you know."

"Thanks Paolo. Call me again sometime."

"I call you all the time."

"You know what I mean."

She had said that to him so many times before, but finally Paolo knew just what she meant. She was going to use him, and he was going to love it.

40. BUMP IN THE NIGHT

Rabbit shouldn't have poured those last two drinks.

He should have put the phone away an hour ago.

He should drag himself to bed before he got into any real trouble.

Instead he scrolled his feeds. Twitter, FriendZone, Insta, News. Everywhere he went he found an enemy. It was an endless loop of ever-shortening updates. He switched between them faster and faster. The Times had done a trend piece on teleportation. Highbrow clickbait designed to stir the socials up.

The story was about Rizon Brocations. Dudes were hiring Hands overseas and spending the entire day as them. They'd do this as a pack, seven or eight guys all connecting to Chiang Mai, Beruit, Odessa. They'd tear up the town from the comfort of their flop house. All the partying with none of the hangovers. All the cheap sex with none of the STDs. This was Rizon's latest innovation—build an overseas posse, get your bros together, and fuck shit up.

Albie Hammel got the kid gloves treatment throughout the article. Instead of calling it exploitation and appropriation, the *Times* called Brocations an exciting collision of culture with the potential for opening the eyes and ears of a usually unreceptive demographic. Hiring sex workers to cruise for tourists was described as an enlightening window into our barest desires.

To Rabbit it sounded like getting fucked twice.

They published this for the hate reads. Well done *NYT*.

Why else would Rizon get a pass for digital slavery? If this was Rabbit, he'd be up on the cross. Peared strictly enforced a no solicitation policy. The internet was indeed dark and full of terror, and Rabbit was smart enough to steer clear of prostitution on his platform. That door only led to the feds. Yet it seemed that the anointed of Sand Hill lived by different rules.

He decided to look at this another way. Albie was setting himself up to fall from such great heights. It had been a dozen years since the Uber scandals. Albie was fourteen when Travis turned from tech god to albatross. While Kleiner remembered, Albie would not. The play here was separating Albie from his herd. Once he was out on his own, he'd just need to have his buttons pushed and a camera on him. That little shit would seed his own demise. Rabbit was sure of it.

He had once been a little shit himself.

Rabbit could see it clearly now. Together needed to rot from the bottom up. Turn the friendly service into a cesspool of anxiety and shit pairing. Rizon was well on its way to creating its own problems. Let them think they are crushing it, then a well-timed headshot would bring it all down.

He swiped his apps closed. One by one, his half-formed rants disappeared into the ether. Finally, there was his messenger app. His ex, Diana was up. It had been ninety days since he last broke down and asked to see the dog. That had gotten nasty fast. Tonight, he had almost asked again, but he was too tired for the accompanying fight. He'd get the dog in a month when she went to Tahoe.

He backed out of that conversation and pulled up Omar. He wanted to share his brilliant revelation with him. He started to type, but his spelling was so bad that auto correct didn't know what he was saying.

Smarten up asshole.

Go to bed before you hurt yourself.

God knows you are trying your damnedest to.

Stop before you manage to aim the gun at your foot.

He plugged the phone in and locked it.

Rabbit staggered into his king bed. He reached for a dog that wasn't there. Then there was just the darkness.

41. FRIENDO

Rabbit walked into the Astro Burger on Santa Monica Blvd. His eyes went straight to the menu. He knew Frank Meyers was sitting in the corner booth on the right. He wanted to get his order in before acknowledging him.

Rabbit ordered a double bacon avocado cheeseburger, fried zucchini sticks, and a large chocolate milkshake. Frank had high cholesterol and had switched to veggie burgers years ago. He was also constantly fighting his weight. Rabbit on the other hand, could use the protein. Food had become a secondary thought and he needed to pack it back on.

He waited until after he finished his order before looking over. There was Frank, alright. That stupid fucking goatee of his. Rabbit started to walk towards him and then his phone rang. Another stunt. In the car, Rabbit had programmed his phone to call himself in five minutes. He pretended it was a very important call and stepped outside to talk to no one. All the while he kept an eye on the Now Serving board. His "call" would end moments after his number came up and his food was ready.

Ten minutes later, Rabbit sat down in the booth. He made sure to open the burger wrapper up, letting the sauce run over his fingers. The air stank of onions and bacon. He lifted the titanic burger up and took a massive bite. Bits of shredded lettuce fell onto his red plastic tray. Still chewing, he looked over at Frank.

"So?"

"I'll wait until you're done."

"Sorry Frank, that was the office. I'm going to need to cut this short. Afraid we're going to have to eat and talk, friendo."

Rabbit opened his milk shake up and dunked a zucchini stick into the cup. He scooped iced chocolate out and bit the stick in half. He dipped the rest of it in ranch dressing.

"Rabbit, we know you are up to something."

"Uh huh. I'm always up to something. Like this burger. Man, I missed this place. Remember how we used to come here for lunch? You used to love the chili fries. How's the veggie burger?"

"It's fine. Rabbit quit fucking around before you cross a line."

"What are you talking about?"

"Elliott doesn't know what a snake you are, but I do. You are fucking with us. I'm telling you to back off before we strike back."

"I'm fucking with you? Me?" Rabbit laughed and sucked on his straw. "Aren't you the guys that cloned my product and took your name from my tagline? I'm fucking with you. That's rich."

"You've been live for what—eighteen months now?"

"Something like that."

"And in all that time, you ever have user sessions go viral?"

"A few here and there. Our users respect what takes place between an Eye and a Hand. A Pair is a special bond, Frank. Why?"

"Yeah, that's what I thought too. Once you form a—what is it, consciousness? You have an obligation to keep that private unless both parties agree. Right?"

Rabbit took the last bite of his burger. He started to lick the pink sauce off his fingers.

"That's how it works for us, but that's a problem for you guys, huh? I've had quite a few funny ones forwarded to me. Those poor Hands, getting played for fools. If that happened to me, I'd hang up and never try you again."

"I think you're our problem."

"Well, Together is definitely mine. It's like someone went to my property and copied everything. The lawn, the garage, the garden, the house, the furniture. Only then they fill it with a bunch of assholes who pretend they designed the joint. I can't imagine why I'm the bad guy here, but you spin whatever bullshit you want, Frank. Tell everyone what a horrible boogieman I am. Meanwhile you just keep on copying my every move. I'm sure people who take a closer look will see exactly what's going on."

"Rabbit, you're not bulletproof. Back off or there will be trouble for you."

"That's quite a threat Frank. Good thing I'm recording this." Rabbit tapped his breast pocket. "You know, in case I catch a bullet. That way the cops will know exactly where to look."

"It's a figure of speech, asshole."

"I know friendo." He pointed a zucchini stick at Frank. "Keep on threatening me. You are so good at it."

"Nothing about you is clean, Rabbit. Don't think I can't bring you down again."

"Time's up Frank. Here's a piece of advice for you. Copying the outside doesn't mean the machinery inside works the same. Stop pointing fingers and take a look within. If you can't manage your community, maybe you shouldn't be in this business. There's a lot of power in Pairs. Not everyone is good enough to wield it. Your masters at Thorn should have spent some of that $80 million on brains. Instead they got you and your empty threats."

Rabbit got up, milk shake in hand, and left the booth. His tray remained behind, covered in greasy wrappers, bread crumbs, and stained napkins.

42. GO TIME

The heat was on Kendra. She had enjoyed years of founder's perks—private jets, big salary, and an unusual amount of control over the company. She got the special treatment because she was supposed to be special. Only the numbers were the numbers. It didn't take a genius to see her time was running out. Kendra knew what was coming. Her board was going to replace her with someone cheaper and more efficient. It was in the company's DNA, her DNA. That was going to be a problem. Kendra was highly leveraged. She'd taken her money from tech and put it in real estate. Single digit returns didn't do it for her, so she decided to develop her own land. She was halfway through a project that consumed 75% of her compensation.

She couldn't afford to be fired, at least not yet. She picked up her mobile and dialed Malcolm.

"Hello?"

"Malcolm, it's Kendra."

"Clever Kendra. How are you?"

"Lovely. I've got some wonderful news for you."

"I hope it's about our enterprise."

"Why else would I call you darling?"

"You've called me many, many things, but darling is not one of them. So, what is it?"

"We are operationally ready. Do you have something lined up?"

"Yes, I've got something. Something light that pays. A million for the job, plus another million as a success fee."

"That's all my end?"

"It is."

"Good. Let me know who Paolo should get in touch with."

"Is he ready for this sort of thing?"

"Oh yes. We have him. Hook, line, and sinker."

"Excellent."

Kendra hung up and smiled. Two million was a good number. She needed to cut Paolo in for half, then the rest would go towards construction. Once Paolo took the money, she'd feel better about him. It would fill his belly, but also make him criminally bound to their conspiracy. While she had him trapped in a spiderweb of infatuation, rough sex, and blackout drugs, that wouldn't hold forever. Paolo was no dummy. Without the money, the rush of the illicit would fade. That threat went away the second he took their cash. After that, there'd be no escaping. Thank God, too. Kendra was stretched thin. Between this job, some savings, and a golden parachute, she'd have enough to handle a worst-case scenario, but she needed more. Kendra had miscalculated badly with NAM and needed to make up for lost time.

43. JOB DESCRIPTION

She was wearing a black dress, enormous sunglasses, and a wide brimmed hat. She carried shopping bags in one hand and a small leather purse in the other. To an untrained eye, she looked like half the women in the hotel. Generic, upscale shopper, heading back from the boutiques.

Paolo recognized her immediately as the woman from that night.

They made quick eye contact. She continued strolling through the lobby. He got up and followed her to the elevator. She handed him her shopping bags and pressed the up button. They ascended in silence. Paolo examined the skin of her neck. No marks or bruises. The shallow yellow from that night had been erased and replaced by the light of the sun. The elevator stopped on eleven. She stepped out; he followed her down the hall. The carpet pattern was a maze of red and gold interlocking diamonds. At 11015, she took out her key card and opened the door.

Paolo paused for a moment, afraid to cross the threshold. Last time he trusted this woman he lost an evening of his life. Then again, he was back because he wanted that to happen again.

"Get inside."

He did as he was told. The door clicked shut behind him.

"You can put the bags on the other bed. Let's talk about this job."

Paolo put the bags down, turned, and faced her. "I need a name first. Your real one."

"Monica."

"Monica?"

"Just Monica."

"I'm just Paolo."

"You are a whole lot more than just Paolo."

He smiled and looked across at her. "Just like you're a lot more than Monica."

"Sometimes, but not today. This is business," she said trying to keep on track.

"Before business, I need to know a few things. Otherwise there can't be business."

"Go on," Monica ordered.

"Were you in on it?"

"Of course, I was in on it."

"Were you drugged?"

"Yes."

"Same as me?"

"Same as you."

"Who drugged you?"

"I did it myself."

Paolo looked at her cockeyed. "Why?"

"That's how it works. I'll save you the questions. Yes, you hurt me. No, not badly. Yes, I knew what they were going to do with us. Part of me likes it, part of me does it because that's the gig. Now we need to talk about this job. No job, no next time. You understand?"

"Yes."

"This should be a simple enough task. The city of Lagos wants to build a new stadium as part of a revitalization project." She opened a folder, pulled out a map, and pointed to a circled area on it. "They want to use land that one of our clients owns. Our client is planning to build a marina and hotel there and is not being fairly compensated for the land. We need to turn the public against the stadium idea and get it killed."

Paolo stood over her, leaned in and asked, "What's the angle?"

"Oil prices are low, so Nigeria is broke. They owe China a lot of money. Anti-Chinese resentment is running high. You are going to start a riot and ransack a Chinese-owned block. Afterwards, the Chinese community will demand an apology. Make sure the Nigerians are too pissed off to let their government apologize."

He reached around her, a finger tracing the circle on the map, his chest brushing against her back. "What does that do for your client?"

She stepped away and turned towards him. "Chinese money is going to build the stadium. No apology, no stadium. Our client waits a month, spreads some money around, and they get cleared to break ground on their project."

"So, you just need one big riot to smash up a bunch of boutiques?"

"That's it." She closed the folder and handed it to him. "This has all the background you need for the job."

He took it from her and placed it in his laptop bag. "Monica, why do I want to do it again?"

"For the purge. Every bad thing about you comes to the surface and is washed away. You wake up the next day feeling empty. That's why we wait until after a job. It drains us of the horrible things we've done, so that we can go out there and do more of them."

"That doesn't last, does it?"

"No. At some point you do it just to turn yourself off."

"You there yet?"

"I was, then we found you and Kendra." She walked towards the door and opened it. "It's time for you to go, Paolo."

Paolo lingered for a moment, then kissed her on the lips. It was a quick tentative kiss for a couple who had done so much more before. She smiled, then disappeared behind her glasses. The door shut, and he was back out in the hall.

44. TWINNING

Guy and Girl Sam walked into Rabbit's office. They handed him a legal-sized printout. Rabbit put his coffee down, picked it up, and turned the paper on its side. It was covered with tables full of numbers, dollar signs, and percentages. The print was tiny, and the headings were all written in a code he didn't understand. He'd never seen them present something so raw and unpolished before. It was either great or horrible news. He looked up at them.

"What is this?" Rabbit asked.

"It's the first pass of our analysis," she answered.

"I can't read it."

"We know, but we wanted to share it right away."

"Ok, so good or bad?"

"Very good."

"Really?"

"You see here?" Girl pointed to a highlighted row. "That's the universe of Together users. Approximately 300,000. Eighty-five percent of them are in the US. Ten percent are overseas, and are you ready for this?"

Rabbit looked up with a slightly insulted look. "Of course, I am."

"The last 5% are ours. They are what Tijuana is using."

"So, either we've got too many people in TJ or Together

doesn't have enough users." Rabbit said.

"Both." they answered.

"How many of their accounts are active?" Rabbit picked up the printout and scanned it, absorbing the numbers.

"It's hard to say since they've been live for less than 90 days, but we are seeing huge churn rates from the earliest cohorts," she said.

"Is Omar working?" he asked.

"Yes, but we can't say exactly how well."

"Why?"

"Because we think they've paired with 65% of Together users already."

Rabbit leaned back in his chair, truly surprised for the first time in this conversation. "Get the fuck out of here."

"They are doing too good a job. We think they'll get detected if they keep it up at that rate," Girl Sam said.

"No shit. I sat down with Frank Meyers earlier this week. He thinks I'm fucking with them. Looks like I am doing more than that. I'm owning them. How big is Rizon?"

"Half the size, but a lot more active. We've laid off of them like you asked. Are you sure we don't want to devote our excess capacity to that network?"

"No. Albie's going to blow that company up on his own. What's the money look like?"

She pointed to figures in the lower left corner of the spreadsheet. "We think Together is spending $1.5 million a month on marketing. It costs them $10 for a new user, but when you factor in churn that cost shoots up to $80 per active user. That's a conservative estimate. Omar costs us $400k a month.

"So how much you thinking to bleed them dry?"

"If we only focus on them, and these trends continue? Maybe

it costs us $5-10 million?" she said.

"Seems like a bargain. Polish this up, check everything three times, and get a proper presentation on my calendar."

"Um, Rabbit?" Guy finally spoke.

"Yes, Guy?"

"You don't want actual files, do you? Last I heard this was between you, us, and Sonny."

"Jesus, right. Just check the numbers out and come back to me once you are sure."

He watched them scuttle out and head back to their tiny temporary office. He couldn't imagine spending that much time with one person. Even if that person was your twin. He also couldn't imagine answering to Guy or Girl, their given first names. Sam was their middle name. Rabbit wasn't sure what their last name was. They weren't on his payroll. He supposed he could ask them someday, but what fun would that be? Better to idly speculate on something that had almost no importance to him.

His mind went back to the problem at hand. Together was doing better marketing in the US than Peared. They did have the benefit of the Silicon Valley machine behind them. Rabbit had no idea how many of their users were organic and how many they had paid for. If churn was really that high though, they wouldn't have a prayer of growing their base organically. They'd have to start spending a lot more to bring in new users. Growth was everything in the Valley. If you're not growing, you're dying.

Rabbit sprung his traps while Together's attention was focused on launch. Now that it was live, they would start to scrutinize their user behavior. It was only a matter of time before Frank and Elliott figured out Rabbit's game, then they'd respond. Move one would be blocking Omar's Army. Move two would be copying Peared's overseas success.

It was going to get a lot harder to ruin Together. Then again, Rabbit was making money and could play this game forever. All he needed to do was make life miserable until Together ran out of cash and couldn't raise more.

45. LAYER FAKE

Paolo watched the video. Two Chinese men were in a warehouse. Behind them were boxes labeled Prada, Gucci, Fendi, Dolce. The older man owned the place and merchandise. The younger man was new in town. In Mandarin, he called the older man uncle and asked him how the business worked. They talked and loaded boxes into the back of a white Toyota pickup. The conversation was very casual, and their tone was familiar. Uncle lit a cigarette and explained to the younger man how everything he saw here was fake. It all came from China. Perfect replicas. Sure, some buyers could tell the difference, but not the Nigerians. They were unsophisticated. More interested in what the label read than checking the craftwork. No one here understood proper stitching or what the hologram was supposed to look like.

These people are idiots, animals. He went on. No one ever asked for serial numbers or called to authenticate merchandise. He held a bag up. This cost me $100. I sell it for $1000. The store sells it for $2000. Never a complaint, never a question.

We Chinese will own Nigeria in another decade, he said.

Paolo watched the video looking for anything out of place. He kept pausing and Googling. The license plate was right. The power sockets looked correct. The boxes looked right. It felt authentic enough for the job. He turned to his vendor, Mack, who also played the younger man in the video.

"Do Chinese people speak differently in Nigeria?" Paolo asked.

"How the fuck should I know? What I do know is that when people from the mainland talk to each other, they all speak like they're back home. Doesn't matter where you are."

"How'd you get the outside to look like Nigeria?"

Mack turned and looked out the back of the warehouse. He was staring at an alleyway in Downey, California. There was a chain link fence in the background and railroad tracks past that.

"Dude, you're in Los Angeles. The FX and props were the easiest part of the video."

Paolo reached into his bag and pulled out a manila envelope with $5000 in it. He handed it to the man who gave him a USB stick in return. In an hour, Paolo would VPN into a Nigerian IP address and post the video on YouTube and Reddit. After that, he'd send $500 to someone in Bangladesh who'd make sure that the video generated tens of thousands of views and upvotes overnight.

When he woke in the morning, the video had gone viral. In Lagos it was 3:00 pm on Sunday and anger was running high. Paolo put the second part of his plan into action. He backdoored into Peared and pulled up the administrator console, God Mode. There were 10,000 Pairs in Nigeria, most of them in Lagos. He was on the hunt for several Eyes he had been monitoring. They were merchants who used runners as Hands to conduct business around the city. Instead of having to fight through traffic for meeting after meeting, these guys had figured out they could buy their flunkies AR glasses and send them out in their place.

He found Ibrahim who was a distributor in Yaba. Paolo put his AR glasses on and faced a concrete wall that showed nothing. He took control of Ibrahim's feed and connected them together.

"Ibrahim, this is a friend." Paolo said in a garbled voice.

"I don't know you. How did you do that?"

"Don't worry about that. Tonight at 10:00 pm, I want you to click on this link. You'll see live footage of Tunji Awojobi Street in VI. Two diesel tankers are going to explode on opposite ends of the block. All the store windows will be blown out. Police and fire will take their time getting there. Have your runners loot the stores."

Paolo dropped the feed. He repeated this process eight more times. Some would do it, others would not, but they would get the word out. There would be looting.

He then found his two Evil Eyes. These men he had paid very close attention to. He had paired with both of them earlier in the week and sent 50,000 NGN to their mobiles as a sign of good faith. They were tasked with finding Hands that would steal the trucks and put them at each end of the block. The first had paired with twenty people already that day. He was searching for a sucker. The other was online but quiet. He was connected to a Hand. Paolo opened their feed. The Hand was sitting in the cab of a truck already.

Good. He liked efficient sociopaths.

He'd check back in just before 10:00 pm. He still needed to get someone to puncture each tanker and light them up. Paolo was going to be the Evil Eye that handled that job. He started looking online for someone who had a motorbike and was really pissed off.

46. CONFIRMATION

Monica took the Mac Book out of her bag and placed it in the middle of the Sunseeker's aft deck table. She sat down next to their client and tunneled into a virtual machine on the other side of the world, then opened a web browser. She reached into her small leather purse and pulled out a folded piece of paper. Her sharp black fingernails slowly typed the written address into her browser.

A moment later, a grainy video of Tunji Awojobi Street in Victoria Island came up. She opened the video to full screen and tilted it so that the client had the best view. The street was quiet—a couple parked cars and a few second-story lights. Shops closed early on Sunday night.

They watched as two diesel tankers pulled up and blocked both ends of the small street. A man wearing AR glasses got out of one cab and disappeared into the shadows.

A few minutes later a motorcycle appeared next to a tanker. A man got off the bike, unscrewed the hose hookup, then pulled a lever. Diesel began to flood the street. He biked to the other end of the street and repeated the process. The bike returned to the center of the street. The man lit two Molotov cocktails. He threw one towards the north tanker and one towards the south. As soon as the second left his hand, the bike took off down an alley. A moment later there was a massive yellow flash and the street became invisible.

Monica smiled; she knew that Paolo would get it done.

They waited five minutes as the flames and smoke began

to dissipate. Men wearing hats and scarves began appearing on the street. Some had AR glasses on, many carried bags. Monica watched as they went to work. Men threw stuff out into the street. The guys with the AR glasses pointed at what to take and what to leave as others filled the bags. They worked quickly, extracting the most valuable items before smoke or other looters could ruin the merchandise. The first wave of men disappeared as a mob began to fill the street. Sirens rang out in the distance.

Monica shut off the feed.

"Satisfied?" she asked the man.

"Yes," he answered.

"We'll expect a wire on Monday."

"You'll have it."

"White Bordeaux?" Monica offered.

"Sounds wonderful."

She walked inside the cabin and opened a bottle on ice.

Across town, Paolo shut his equipment off and began packing up. It was hardly the elegant centaur solution he had first thought up, but it was effective. Each piece had been handled in a modular fashion and at an arms-length from himself. All the payments were done from burner phones using crypto. None of his interactions on Peared registered on the live network. As a rule, God Mode didn't log data. Mack was the only person he directly interacted with and that was unavoidable. That video was key to the second part of the job. There needed to be no apologies.

47. SIXTY-EIGHT GUNS

Em watched that rat weasel slink down the hallway. She'd been waiting all weekend to confront him, playing the conversation out in her head, unable to put it aside. She didn't know why she put faith in people. She hated how easily they dismissed potential threats. Why couldn't they see the world the way she did? Some people weren't smart enough to see all the angles—Em could forgive that. What she couldn't forgive were the people who saw all the angles but didn't have the spine to nip the bad ones in the bud.

Sonny had lied to her. It was a lie of omission, but that didn't make it any better. What bothered her most wasn't this lie, it was wondering what else was out there. When she wasn't spending Sunday having imaginary conversations with Sonny, she was wondering what other shit Rabbit had gotten them into. She thought Sonny and Paolo were with her as backstops. Instead, they just told her what she wanted to hear and then never followed through on it. Fucking pointless.

It was showtime. She got up from her desk and followed Sonny down the hall.

"Sonny, can we talk for a minute?" she asked, stepping between him and the door to his office.

"Of course Em, what can I do for you?"

"I met a Peared employee this weekend. It was the funniest thing—she said she worked for our call center in Tijuana. I told her that was impossible, we didn't believe in call centers, and we certainly didn't have an office in Mexico. She looked at me like I had two heads and then asked if I really worked at Peared. It was quite an odd back and forth. Eventually she showed me a picture of her, Rabbit, and yourself." Em paused for a moment, watching Sonny's face to see how he was going to play this. She continued. "She's hot—I can see why you'd take a picture with her. The problem is, she's also a real social climber. Will say anything to get ahead. In fact, she told me exactly what she does for us."

"I see." Sonny mustered.

"So, I'm listening to her and getting angrier and angrier as she tells her story. At first, I'm mad that we are doing something that's galactically stupid, but then I start getting mad at myself for not knowing about this; finally I realize where my anger really belongs. It's at you." Her sharp fingernail jabbed him in the chest. "What the fuck happened to sharing information, Sonny?"

"I decided not to in this case."

"Why?"

"I don't know."

"You don't know? What are you four years old?"

Sonny ran his hands through his short-cropped hair and let out a long sigh. "I was stretched thin, trying to juggle a facility build-out and my work here. Telling you would have just created all sorts of drama."

"As compared to now? Two hundred people in Mexico trolling our competition was exactly the sort of stupid, narrow thinking I was trying to prevent in the first place. Only I can't do it if my 'allies' act just as stupid and shortsighted as fucking Rabbit. This is the sort of decision he needed to be checked on."

Sonny took a moment, weighing his words before picking a side. "Em, I work for Rabbit. I report to Rabbit. He pays me. This is his company. It's not yours and it's not mine. I should have never created an expectation that I would share confidential information with you. That was my mistake and I regret that."

"This is going to bite us in the ass. It's always the stupid fucking shortcuts that cause all the problems later. Tell me this, is there any other dumb shit going on?"

"Not that I know of. I suppose you are going to fly off the handle on Rabbit, then I'll get dragged into it?"

He motioned for her to step aside so he could enter his office. She stood firm.

"No, I'm going to talk to Paolo and see what other shenanigans we've got going on around here. After that, I'll figure out what I want to do. No point in raising hell if I'm the only sensible person at Peared. This is a great example of why I should stick to freelance projects. Hang around people for more than three months and they'll disappoint you."

Sonny leaned in until they were eye to eye. He spoke slowly in a strong but emotionless tone.

"Em, you have a much higher opinion of yourself than you ought to. Like I said, this isn't your company. It's Rabbit's."

"And you have far too low an estimation of the damage he can do."

"We'll see," Sonny said as he brushed her aside and walked through the doorway of his office.

"Oh, we will," Em said to Sonny and his door as he closed it on her.

48. BLOW UP

"Hello."

"Paolo, it's Rabbit."

"Hey boss, what's up?"

"You tell me."

Paolo froze; a chill ran down his spine. It was the day after the Nigerian job. Paolo was in LA, but everyone thought he was up north. He'd been careful not to be seen, but Peared had two hundred employees and almost all of them knew who he was. Had he been spotted at LAX? Maybe checking into his hotel or out grabbing lunch? He was staying in Covina, far east of the office, but the freeways were never empty and eyes where everywhere.

"What's bothering you, Rabbit?"

"The fucking numbers, Paolo. You know, your direct responsibility. I shouldn't have to ask you what's up, you should be coming to me. Our average revenue per user is in an ugly decline. Tell me why."

"A couple things. It's seasonal. Spending dies down after Christmas, so advertisers dial back. CPCs will pick up again soon. The other part are these new users. They're less engaged. I've got the AI figuring out how to get our hooks into them."

"You know Paolo, some people might buy that bullshit, but I don't. You picked the path of least resistance. We got a bunch of poor people crammed ten to an apartment passing around gear that's three generations old. No one wants to advertise to slums. Get off your ass and find us some better users."

Rabbit only thought in one direction. Relationships boiled down to what can someone do for Rabbit, and why the fuck weren't they doing more of it. If you were top of mind, you were in trouble. Paolo usually said nothing. It was better to take the abuse, let the man run out of steam, and tell him what he wanted to hear. More often than not, Rabbit would move on to the next target and forget all about you.

Paolo wasn't in a shit-taking mood today.

"What am I using to find those users?" he asked Rabbit.

"Your fucking brain. You know that thing between your ears that used to be worth something."

"One man can only do so much, Rabbit."

"One man? There're eighty of you up at NAM running an AI that's supposed to be able to do the work of a thousand people."

"It is doing that work."

"Not very well."

"I told you a month ago that we were tapped out. You remember that conversation? The one where I said this was going to happen? The one where I told you that unless the product got some new features we were going to level off? You remember that, don't you? If not, here's a refresher. After I told you the product was stale and leaving revenue on the table, I then told you that you needed to spend real money on marketing. Let Em do her job. Our AI is optimized for efficiency, not creativity. It takes the people who like our service and finds more people like it. What it cannot do is sell third tier shit to first class users. Do you remember that?"

"No."

"Really? It was a forty-five minute conversation. I was pretty fucking passionate Rabbit. By the end I thought you understood. But we'll try this again. We compete for attention. Peared works well for poor people because it's free and it pulls them out of their miserable lives for an hour. You want rich people? You want those high-end users that advertisers pay for? Then give me a fucking product that can compete with Apple, BMW, and Netflix. Give me something that looks like it was designed next year, not three years ago."

"We don't have the money for that."

"Really? That's funny because I know what we bring in the front door. If you don't have the money, then something stupid is going out the back. I know you think if you press hard enough, people will find a magical solution that doesn't involve opening up your wallet. That's not happening this time. We've squeezed everything we can from this platform. If you want better results, invest in the product and the presentation. I'm sick of carrying the load for the rest of you assholes."

The phone went dead. Rabbit had hung up on him. Paolo shrugged and tossed it on his bed. If that asshole didn't want to hear the truth, there was nothing Paolo could do about it.

49. DOUBLE MOVE

Rabbit strode down the jogging trail, an angry white man in a black suit. He cut past little dogs on leashes and housewives in yoga pants. He was beyond bullshit. His money was flowing in the right direction. How dare Paolo question his priorities.

He'd put $14 million into Peared. It was a loan from himself to the company. Now, he wanted to be repaid. For the last three months, Peared cut him a check for $1.5 million dollars. In another six months he'd have his money back. The rest of the profits were going to fund Omar's Army.

If everything went according to plan, Together would go broke the same month the loan was repaid. At that point, he could listen to Paolo and upgrade the service. Paolo wasn't wrong, he just didn't see the entire chessboard. Peared did need a new coat of paint. It could use a couple new bells and whistles. It needed a real marketing budget. Now was not the right time for any of that. This was war time, and he needed to dictate the terms of battle.

Peared could not compete on product or presentation. While Rabbit had invented teleportation, he didn't have the sophistication or polish the Valley did. Fighting on features and functions meant losing. He needed to keep everything in the trenches.

In the Valley, companies would not expand until they got the core experience right and found a passionate userbase. Once they had that, they would build on their success. If the core experience was rotten, the company had no chance.

Rabbit needed to mow every new Together user down until they stopped coming out of the trenches. Once that happened, the Valley would look at its wasted investment, Peared's crappy overseas users, and they'd abandon the space. Then and only then would Rabbit invest in his own product.

Still Paolo had no business telling Rabbit how to run his. Paolo's job was to do what Rabbit told him and to keep his opinions to himself.

His phone rang. It was Frank Meyers. He dismissed the call. It rang again.

"This better be good Frank. I'm in the middle of something important."

"Something important, Rabbit?"

"Yeah, business. You wouldn't know what that was."

"Are you going into dog walking or are you trying to find another rich divorcee to marry? If it's marriage, find one that hides her cheating better."

Rabbit looked around. He couldn't see Frank, but a man wearing AR glasses, khaki pants, and a black polo shirt was approaching him.

"Why are you following me around Frank? Don't have anything better to do?"

"I'm just coming by to share some news with you. We just acquired Anslem Devices."

"Who the fuck are they?"

"Don't play dumb, Rabbit. All those insults about copying you really got under my skin. You are a talented guy Rabbit, a major asshole, but still a talented guy. The thing is that you are a derivative thinker. Your playbook is taking one thing and recasting it in another space. You don't invent anything. You just see angles. So, I thought about it some. How the fuck did you come up with Peared? There wasn't an Isaac Newton under an apple tree moment. That's not something you do. Then I had my big aha! You copied someone else and put your own twist on it."

Rabbit swallowed hard. The man in the AR glasses was within fifty feet of him. He was holding a document, waiting patiently. Frank continued.

"I'm sorry I couldn't do this in person. I'm not a registered process server, but what's great about Together is that I can see the look on your face. It's priceless. Are you shitting out a prune or wondering what's coming next?"

The man approached and handed Rabbit the document.

"Rabbit Wilson, you have been served."

Rabbit opened the light blue cover and read the first page.

"Next time, think before opening that big mouth of yours Rabbit. We bought the company whose code you stole. Now we are suing you for intellectual property theft. Oh, the irony. This makes us the original and you a petty fucking plagiarist. See you in court friendo."

50. MASTRO'S OCEAN CLUB

Monica looked stunning.

Coral dress, gold filigree bracelet, tanned bronzed skin. Paolo gazed across the table into her dark brown eyes. He wanted to drown in them. They should be walking the beach in Kailua, not sitting in Malibu with sadists.

She smiled back at him. He felt their chemistry. It was bigger than the job, capable of living outside the shadow cast on their relationship. He wondered how real it was. Was it a work or something else? He fell in love with a girl once, only to discover they were both in love with the drugs.

Chemistry is dirty that way.

Malcolm was doing his best to stay in the background. It was a nearly impossible task for so large a man. His restraint surprised Paolo. Usually these blowhards made everything about themselves, but tonight it felt like Malcolm and Kendra were at another table.

Was Malcolm shrewder than he let on? Did he really want Kendra? Maybe Monica and Malcolm were running a game on both of them.

If so, they were very smooth operators.

At this point, Paolo didn't care. The anticipation was killing him. He felt like a kid. That no one even hinted at it, made it all the more exciting.

Two dozen oysters arrived on a silver platter. Miniature pitchers of garnish were buried in the crushed ice. Tiny utensils placed like compass points. The waiter popped a bottle of Veuve. The foursome took a moment to toast their enterprise. Paolo braced himself for Malcolm to ruin the moment. It never came.

Kendra was a vision in white. He realized that she'd always been a distant beacon. Big sister, boss lady, older crush. He'd never be able to do this without her, and they'd never get together on their own. Only here in this complicated web could they cross boundaries without breaking their relationship. He needed her, so he could step off the cusp of nothingness.

She would keep him safe in the dark.

Kendra looked over at him, dipping her glass slightly. It was the closest anyone would come to an acknowledgement, but it was all Paolo needed to see.

He was ready to empty himself and arise anew.

51. SLATE

He opened the French doors to the Pacific. Monica stood naked in the sand. She was smoking a cigarette, holding a small white cup of steaming black coffee. Paolo made out a line of goose-bumps running down her shoulders and over her thighs. The ocean was the smell of salt and the steady crash of waves. Fog consumed the view, hiding the never-ending sea from their sights. Somewhere a gull cried out. It would not scavenge until the sun burned through. Paolo had a fluffy white towel wrapped around his waist and another draped over his shoulders. The wet January chill seeped through the slate deck stones. He shivered.

They were in a small white cottage built into the side of a hill. The master bedroom opened onto the deck and beach. The rest of the house was upstairs, just a living room, kitchen, and a small guest room. Such a modest home for so prime a location.

The house was empty and spotless. Like they had never been there at all.

Paolo looked to the right, they were on a small cove. He could make out the sea meeting rocks and scrub, a few hardy trees dug in to a creek. To the left were a couple hundred yards of sand, then a cliff butted into the ocean. Everything else was lost to the mist.

He had no idea where he was or what time it was.

Monica turned and walked towards him. He held the towel out and took her coffee cup. She looked up into his eyes. Her pupils were white and clear. She ran her hands down his sides. There wasn't a scratch.

"Do you remember anything about last night?" she asked.

"No," he answered, running his hand over the towel covering her back.

"Neither do I."

"Do you know this place?" Paolo asked as he looked around.

"No."

"Neither do I."

"My mobile is gone. There's no TV in the house, no clocks, no calendars. A pathway leads up the hill." Monica walked towards the French doors.

"What do you think is there?"

She turned in the direction of the path and gave him a smile. "A gassed-up SUV with the keys in it and our things in back. Malcolm has done this before."

"Done what?"

"Left me in another world."

"I don't want to leave, Monica."

"Neither do I. We'll stay another night. Just you and me this time."

52. YOU GOTTA WALK

The elevator opened. Em stepped out into the parking garage. She scanned the rows of cars looking for the bright blue Porsche with the tinted windows. Sonny was inside, and they needed to talk. She found his car in a far corner of the garage. He didn't like parking too close to others, always worried about scratches. This conversation would be worse than any scratch across his precious car. Sonny thought Em was a real Chicken Little, but now the sky was falling and she had to tell Sonny it was landing on him. She opened the door and slid into the passenger seat.

"Peared is being sued for intellectual property theft," Em began.

"What?" Sonny gave her a quizzical look.

"Frank Meyers gave me a call. The source code for the AR and VR clients was copied from a surgical training program. It is not a licensed SDK like Rabbit told you."

"Fuck." He smacked the steering wheel with his open palm.

"Fuck indeed, Sonny." She gave him her best 'hate to say I told you so' look. "How much of it is still in there?"

"None of it. We swapped it all out six months in. It didn't play well with the rest of our stack."

"That's good. Damages will be minimal."

"It's not good, Em. Even if there's a settlement, this is a big hit to my reputation and to the reputation of the technology team."

"That's true, but there are ways of compensating for reputation." Em pretended to be interested in her fingernails, fanning them in front of her face, looking at each one as Sonny stared back at her.

"You want me to sell myself?"

Finally, she turned and acknowledged him. "You already have, you just didn't know it at the time. Now that Rabbit cost you, the question is what are you going to do about it?"

"He's cost me twice. First by not selling to Thorn, now my reputation."

Now she followed with the words. "Hate to say I told you so."

"Who is suing us?"

"Well this is where it gets complicated. Together bought the IP. They are bringing the suit."

"Frank Meyers?"

"Yes."

Sonny leaned back, scratched his chin, and stared out the window. "That crafty bastard. I want no part of their fight and you shouldn't either. Ethics aside, and I'm finally having a hard time putting them aside, that is a blood feud. There's no safe harbor there."

"What have I been saying all along? On its own, I could have managed our image through this lawsuit, but combine it with your TJ operation, plus there's also..."

Em trailed off. Nadia Camiso was on her lips, but Sonny didn't need to know about her, at least not at this point. She could probably get Rabbit around two of those problems, but all three? Impossible. Someone was holding Nadia back. If Em found out about her, then so had Meyers and Thorn. It was only a matter of time before they learned about Mexico, too.

"Look Sonny, I'm done. I can't do this anymore."

"Done? What about your options?" Sonny asked.

"Chief Marketing Officer was an experiment. It failed. Managing Rabbit would have been a challenge if we stuck together, but we couldn't do that. I'm going back to my old life. It pays well and doesn't require faith in others. Stock options be damned."

"Em, there aren't many startups with 200 million users. Even if Rabbit is an ass and even if he's getting sued, our chances of cashing out here are better than anywhere else." Sonny tried to convince her as much as himself.

"No, they are not."

"Why do you say that?"

"Because I've done the same analysis that you are about to, and I'm walking. There's more dirt on Peared than the IP theft. If Rabbit tried to sell today, Thorn wouldn't offer him a pot to piss in. Go ahead and ask your friend up there. You are right. This is a blood feud, but Rabbit is beefing in the wrong direction. Thorn hired Frank Meyers specifically to distract Rabbit, and that move just paid off. You think Rabbit is a pain to work with now? Just wait until he's spent two years fighting their lawyers instead of paying damages in arbitration. Our definition of winning is radically different than Rabbit's. This is all personal to him. It's all about his neglected ego. Take your vested options and walk."

"You know what the worst part of this is?"

"What Sonny?"

"Had he just told me upfront, I could have built the stolen clients in four months. This was avoidable."

"What did I tell you about shortcuts? They always bite you in the ass. So, what are you going to do?"

Sonny let out a long sigh. "I don't know. I'll take some

meetings, put out feelers. Vic Khan is starting something up in Pasadena. I always got on well with him." He paused again, and then continued. "Em, I'm sorry I froze you out on Tijuana. It was just easier at the time."

53. BUSINESS CLASS

Kendra walked into the Coffee Bean. Terry Walker was sitting in the back, a green tea next to his iPad. They were on neutral ground, halfway between NAM's headquarters in Los Gatos and Terry's office in Palo Alto. Terry was Kendra's closest friend on NAM's board, which is why she knew he'd swing the axe.

The timing was bad, but was there ever really a good time? The board wasn't interested in Kendra's financial situation, it was interested in NAM's performance, which sucked. She ordered a latte with skim milk then turned to meet her fate.

"Terry, good to see you."

Walker was wearing his everyday uniform, khakis, a pale blue button up shirt, and oxfords. His dirty blonde hair was parted to the side, the same way it had been since he was a teen. He made his style choices in prep school and stuck to them ever since. Minimalism took him young. If you ever wanted to hear Terry talk, ask his opinion on decision fatigue.

He looked up from his iPad, his mouth was drawn tight, his analytical eyes fixed on her. Kendra could tell the decision had already been made. He didn't get up, instead he pointed to the opposite seat.

"Kendra, thank you for coming all the way out here. How was traffic?"

"Fine, Terry. Did you make it down ok?"

"No problems at all."

"Good."

He put his iPad down, pushed his glasses up, and leaned back in his chair. She braced herself.

"Kendra, as you know, the board has a duty to make sure that NAM is being managed optimally. You also know that Walker, Wesley, Sweetman takes a long-term approach to their investments. At the same time, we need to be cognizant of reality."

"Terry, I..."

He held up his hand. "Please, let me continue. This is difficult for me, as I'm sure it will be for you. Kendra, we made an unusual bet on you back in 2017. At the time, machine learning was showing outsized promise. We bet that the field would continue on that pathway and we bet that you were the right person to implement those advances. Things did not turn out that way. The field has stagnated, and you have not demonstrated growth capabilities outside of your core expertise. Today we need to start the process of winding down that bet. It is time to salvage what we can."

It was Kendra's turn to put up her hand. "Enough pussyfooting Terry. Just give it to me."

"You're out."

"That's a mistake, Terry."

"No, it's not, Kendra. We intend to sell NAM off. While you've done a serviceable job of operating it, you failed to achieve the scale necessary for it to be a stand-alone business."

"If you are selling it, then why not leave me on to help with the process?"

"Because you'll be a hinderance to the process and frankly, you cost too much."

"Who will take over?"

"Yuri and Gretchen will step up and run the day to day, but I'll be acting CEO. I hope that you'll be available should I have any questions."

"Of course, Terry."

"We are asking you to resign to pursue other opportunities. I know you are in the middle of a large real estate project. Please name that as the reason. We want you to walk away immediately. You'll receive the company's standard severance package of one week's salary for each year served and we'll make you eligible for COBRA benefits. Unfortunately, most of your later options will price underwater, but you'll do okay on your early grants."

Her face went flush. "Terry, those were massively diluted. This isn't how it's done."

"Kendra, we need to send a message. NAM is a lean mean automation machine. A more generous severance package is out of step with the company's culture. Please hand me your badge."

She began to boil red. "I'm not allowed back in?"

"In time we'll welcome you back as our founder, but right now I think we all need space. I hope you'll make this easy for me, there's a lot to be done."

"Like what?" she asked, wondering how deep the humiliation went.

"There are certain clients we need to let go of. Our association with Rabbit Wilson and Peared is problematic relative to its contribution to EBITDA."

Panic kicked in. "Sell the Peared relationship off to the employees, let them spin it out."

"Kendra, having a copy of our AI with a skilled staff of operators out there would create a lower cost competitor to us and hurt the sale value of NAM."

"There are ways to handcuff that business. Those are good people, let them earn a living."

"We'll do our best to refer those employees to other opportunities. Internally or externally. Kendra, I have to ask you to step out of this now. It's no longer your concern. You need to start thinking about your second act and who will support you when the time is right. Do you understand?"

The question hung in the air, the implications unspoken but all too obvious. Kendra hung her head knowing that she would need Terry to be her bridge back to the Valley.

"I do."

"I'm sorry Kendra, but this is for the best. Now if you will excuse me, I need to get down to Los Gatos."

Terry offered his hand to Kendra and she gave him a perfunctory shake. She didn't get up; instead she stared straight ahead as he walked out of the building. While Walker, Wesley, Sweetman took a long-term approach to their investments, they cut bait faster than anyone else in the Valley. Terry wouldn't have pulled the trigger today if he didn't already have a buyer lined up. Like most VCs, he only acted when all the questions were removed, and the outcome was obvious. This was bad. She knew the axe was coming, but had counted on Paolo's team remaining in place. Malcolm was now her only source of income, and they couldn't do those jobs without God Mode.

Who knows how Rabbit would react once he heard the news. Without NAM he was fucked.

54. STRUCK DOWN

Rabbit looked out from his office onto the floor. Em had given notice this morning. He'd tried to turn her into a house cat, but that was never her. Honestly, he'd squandered her talent. Froze her out and handcuffed her abilities. There was so much she could have done, had it only been peacetime. Instead, they were at war and everything needed to be ugly. That meant the one person at Peared capable of true beauty was expendable. Now Sonny was Peared's only real position of strength. Rabbit would have to tell Sonny about the IP lawsuit soon. That would not go well. The real question was how poorly would it go. Rabbit never took the time to line up potential successors. His choices boiled down to kissing Sonny's ass or throwing darts at the tech org chart. Three guys could conceivably replace Sonny and he knew too little about them.

While Rabbit could walk the wire with the best, the wire was really starting to wobble.

His phone buzzed.

"Hey, Kendra."

"Rabbit, you have a problem."

He ran his hand over his face. "You heard about Em?"

"Huh?"

"She just quit, I thought maybe news reached you."

"No, but this is worse."

Rabbit jerked upright, bracing himself. "What?"

"I got sacked this morning."

"How is that possible?"

"Terry Walker is cleaning house."

"How is that possible?" He repeated himself. "I thought you said they'd give you at least a year."

"They are selling the company. It gets worse for you, they need to drop Peared as a client before selling. Expect a six-month notification soon. You need to handle the Sams before they get called back to the mothership, then you need to find Paolo a new home ASAP."

Rabbit kicked himself. How could he have been so stupid? In all the scenarios he played out, he never thought he'd lose his back office at NAM. He felt like he was going to have a heart attack. Panic set in for the first time in a dozen years. He took a deep breath, sat on the floor, and stared at his shoes.

"Rabbit you there?"

"I'm sorry Kendra. When are you done?"

"I'm already out.

"Tell me you are shitting me. My whole fucking business is at stake here."

"I'm not, that's why I am calling you. You don't know Terry Walker, but he doesn't make moves like this without a clear view of the runway. NAM is as good as sold."

"Has anyone done diligence on you?"

"No, but Terry has our audited financials and enough paper to get a sale to the goal line. He's now the acting CEO. Diligence will only be a matter of time."

"Thorn."

His head began to spin. Sweat ran down his neck. He white knuckled the phone.

"Don't make this about yourself, Rabbit."

"I'm not but putting the screws to me is what you'd call a portfolio synergy."

"Jesus Christ. I just got fired from the company I founded, and you are bringing this back around to you. We'll talk another time when your head isn't up your ass."

His phone went dead. He dropped it and grabbed both arms of his chair. He counted backwards from ten and popped an Ativan he kept in case of emergency. The benzo cavalry was on its way. He looked at his watch and saw his BPMs at 160 and dropping. He wasn't going to die; he just needed to pull himself together.

Rabbit leveled himself with his monitor and pulled up Thorn Capital's portfolio page. They were in every sector of technology. They had to have a company that could pay a premium for NAM. It would come back in a quid pro quo. Automata. IPO'ed three years ago. Fifteen billion market cap. NAM wasn't worth a billion. Easily absorbable.

Fucking Frank Meyers, that puppeteering fuck. Rabbit's Mexican operation looked like chickenshit compared to the pincer that was closing around him. Rabbit realized what the deep end of the pool really looked like.

He was drowning again. His heart rate spiked. Breathe, fucker. Try not to think. *Breathe.*

If only Kendra had called him before he let Em walk. He'd have done anything to keep her. Now Rabbit would have to handle marketing himself while finding a new back office. The fuck was he going to do without that AI? The fuck was going on with his body?

At this point, Peared could back off some of their outlawed tactics, but they still needed FriendZone Rules for optimization and growth. Even if he found another company willing to play dirty, he'd run the same risk of losing them. This had to come in house. That was going to cost him serious money. He'd have to delay his loan repayments or worse, take on investment.

First, he needed to secure Paolo. He was the key to every-thing.

Fuck. Frank got him good. He was seeing stars.

55. ACCELERATOR

Unlike their prior meetups, today was all about practicalities. Kendra's ouster from NAM and its impending sale had thrown their whole enterprise into doubt. There was a window open, but it would shut fast. Paolo still had not developed the process to his liking. He wanted them to be a layer removed from the jobs. Inception was his ideal and he thought he could get there with enough time and testing. Trying that now would be a recipe for disaster.

He'd done Nigeria because it was half a world away and because he wanted to get to Monica. Now that they were together, his appetite for risk was considerably decreased. This felt too high profile, and he didn't like working on US soil. Law enforcement operated on an entirely different level here. They had the sophistication and intelligence to comprehend how a man like Paolo could execute this operation. Catching him would make someone's career and put him in jail for life.

Cyber terrorism was not something to take lightly.

Of the four conspirators, he was the only one hesitant to go for it. After another turn around the room failed to persuade him, Kendra pulled him out to the deck.

"Paolo, I really need this."

"Why, Kendra?"

"I'm running out of money. I thought I'd get a golden parachute from NAM and it didn't happen. No one will give me another loan. I need the money, or my contractors will walk off the job."

"Jesus, why didn't you tell me?"

"Pride I suppose, but I'm telling you now. This is a lot of money, and you already know how you are going to do it. I can see it in your eyes. You have a solution."

"It's not that hard. You find people who look like they could be working together, but they all act alone. None of them will realize something bigger is happening until they are all in the middle of it and it's too late to back out. Once it's over, they'll be scared shitless and go to ground. I know the type that can bury getting played. Even better, they look the part too. Finding them won't be hard. The only hard part is putting the physical assets in place."

"Which Malcolm and Monica said would be taken care of. You won't be working alone here. There's a lot of institutional support for this job. People will protect us. We are doing the department a big solid."

"The money sounds too good to be true."

"Stakes are high. The money is small when you take a long enough view. Please Paolo, I've never asked you for anything."

"No, you never asked, you forced. I wouldn't be here now had you asked."

"I'm sorry for that. This time is different, I'm asking as a friend. Do me this for me. Besides, you need to look at it from your point of view. Two million can make you. We have no idea how Rabbit will move forward."

"I don't want to talk about Rabbit right now. One thing at a time. If I do this, Monica is in the room with me as the other operator. I want insurance. They need to be in as deep as we are."

"That sounds smart. Thank you, Paolo."

"You're welcome."

He looked through the glass doors at Malcolm and Monica.

He had to remind himself that they had not escalated things. Kendra pushed them to find a big job. She was getting desperate and that was making her dangerous. He had to set limits now before she fucked this all up. With her out at NAM, she had nothing to offer them. Keeping her involved was a liability. At the very least, her greed couldn't drive this forward. He'd have to speak with the other two after this job.

"Kendra, I'm never working in the US again. I'll bail you out this time, but your money issues are yours alone. Find a partner, short sell, or get another job. Don't make this your salvation, because it will be gone before you know it. Rabbit is not someone we can bring into this. If he manages to move Peared's operations in house, we are done. There's no way I'm running jobs on his network."

"Construction is almost complete. I won't ask again. You are a life saver."

56. RICOCHET

Rampart, Rodney King, the Zoot Suit Riots. Pick any decade in Los Angeles and you'll find a flashpoint between the LAPD and the citizenry. It was a tale as old as time, and today was no different. Paolo looked out over the city from the rooftop of the Downtown Standard. He took a sip of coffee and watched as Figueroa filled with protestors from Wilshire all the way back to the Staples Center.

Figueroa, the backbone of downtown, had seen crowds like this before. It was the traditional route of the Lakers victory parade. Today, there was no confetti or trophies. This was a test of bodies and wills. He walked over to the other side of the building and looked up Flower. The streets were blocked off, lined with a wall of blue. SWAT teams in riot gear and military grade equipment stood at the ready. The people planned to march past the power centers of the city, its office towers, cultural monuments, and private clubs. At the end they'd occupy Grand Park in front of City Hall.

Reports expected 100,000 protestors. More than 5,000 cops had gathered downtown. Half had been deployed to the scene, the rest had come out on their own. They were under the strict orders not to shoot and not to use force. One more mishap, and control of the department would slip away. After that it would be yet another federal consent decree. As much as they'd hate to lose control of downtown for the day, it was better than being under the feds for another decade.

Paolo checked the time. The march would begin in twenty

minutes. He finished his coffee and went down to his room.

Monica had the TV tuned to the news. Helicopters swirled above broadcasting overhead shots of downtown. The bed was pushed against the wall. In its place, a folding table joined the room desk in an L. Paolo gave her a kiss and turned the monitors on. Two Mac Books came out of his bag. He opened each, connecting them to the bank of monitors. Next to that he placed a 5G modem with a burner SIM in it. He tunneled into God Mode with the first laptop, then the second. They sat shoulder to shoulder, headsets on, and began searching for their Hands.

Paolo felt confident. This job was technically simpler than the Nigerian one. The mission programs were designed to lead the Hands with minimal interaction from the Eyes, but there needed to be more than one operator on hand to converse, threaten, and cajole their Hands to completion. Monica was the perfect accomplice.

The people were massing against a flatbed truck on the corner of Fig and Wilshire. Organizers wrapped their speeches. The truck backed up and the marchers pushed down Wilshire. From there, they'd cut up Flower, past the public library, before turning onto 1st and City Hall. Paolo and Monica watched the TV, waiting for the crowd to stretch itself out.

"Activating Hand one," Paolo said.

"Activating Hand two," Monica replied.

They watched two red dots light up on the south side of downtown. The Hands were making their way down the numbered streets on an intercept course for the protestors.

"Activating Hand three," Paolo said.

"Activating Hand four," Monica replied.

Dots filled the map and began to branch out across the length of the protest route. There were seven Hands broadcasting across the monitors. Paolo kept a close eye on them as they moved towards their destinations. The sequencing of missions was critical, while they were each acting alone and unaware of the others, they all needed to be in position at the same time.

"Monica, hurry number six along. He's lagging."

She pushed a countdown clock onto his glasses. The man began to accelerate, breaking into a quick jog to make up time.

All seven dots on the screen stopped moving. They were in position.

"I'm pushing the next phase. Be ready to manage your Hands. This is where it gets real."

Paolo looked up at the monitors. Some Hands were in parking garages, others in alleyways. One brave soul was in the middle of the concrete plaza at the Bank of America center. Each one was being directed toward an object in their field of vision. He looked over at Monica. Her client was supposed to have dropped duffel bags off last night.

"This is a gun," Hand four said.

"It's filled with blanks. Put your gloves on. Now, you see the money next to it? That's $5,000. You do as I tell you and after this, you'll pick up another bag with $25,000 in it. You don't, and you'll see a cop coming your way. He'll shoot you on sight. What's it going to be?" Monica said.

"Blanks?" he asked.

"Yes. I'm going to start a counter. When it hits zero, you shoot that gun into the air until it runs out of bullets. After that wipe it, drop it, and follow the directions on your glasses. When you find the money, destroy the glasses and disappear. Are we all good, or do I need to call the cops?"

"We are good."

"That's what I thought."

Paolo spoke into his headset.

"They are smoke grenades. Pull the pins and throw them

onto the street. That's all you need to do. After you toss the last one, I'll send you the location of your reward."

"I just pull the pin?"

"Yes, you fucking idiot. Like you do in the games you play all day. Do I need to repeat myself?"

"No."

He pushed a thirty second countdown to all Hands.

"Number two is fleeing. Do you want me to engage?" Monica said.

"No, let him go. It's more important that the rest set their weapons off."

They watched the monitors. Guns were cocked, pins pulled. Hand seven had a speaker with a switch attached to it. Several hands were positioned in parking garages overlooking the march, others were hidden in alleyways behind dumpsters. The countdown dropped to single digits.

"What's this asshole doing?" Paolo asked.

"Your weapon is nothing but blanks. Do not expose yourself, do not aim at the crowd. If you are seen, I will not send you to the money. Do you understand, asshole? Stay the fuck down. That's an order." Monica barked at him.

Downtown LA filled with the sounds of chaos. The rat-a-tat-tat of automatic weapon fire ricocheted off the sides of tightly packed glass skyscrapers; shotgun shells boomed and smoke filled Flower and 3rd. A loud explosion shook the hotel. Number seven's screen went offline. Paolo pushed phase three to all the Hands, then cut the data connection.

"What the fuck happened to seven? I thought this was all staged?"

"I don't know. Rewind and see."

"We aren't recording Monica. Why would we ever capture

this on tape?"

"Then don't look back and never think about seven again."

They turned to the TV news. Overhead video showed that the LAPD had fallen back into a cordon around Grand Park and City Hall. They formed up in ranks four officers deep and stood motionless as the mile-long stream of protestors fled downtown in panic. The message was clear. If you don't like the way we work, then don't look to us for help.

It would be a long time before another group came out to protest.

Paolo packed up. Tomorrow this will be called terrorism, but the reality was that seven trench coat mafia-types had their buttons pushed. For one, it was pushed the wrong way. The rest would take their money and hopefully never speak again. If they did, what would their story be? That the LAPD hijacked their internet and made them fire fake bullets. That wouldn't go very far.

Maybe Alex Jones would listen. Paolo didn't think anyone else would.

57. ONE DOOR OPENS

Sonny used to care about everything. Now he was dead eyes and one-word answers. His body language said it clearly. He was done with this bullshit. Rabbit watched him from his office. Was Sonny already out the door, another defector in a long line of losers, or was he simply giving up? Best case scenario, Sonny was going to stay, but mail it in day after day. At least that would mean the rest of the team was safe. If he had one foot out the door, then Rabbit had a real problem on his hands.

Stealing the Immercast Mafia would be quite the score for someone, and it would leave Peared's cupboard bare. That's how things worked in this town. Techies latched on to good bosses who got them bigger paychecks. When the boss left, they were sure to follow.

Sonny was not going to lie about the stolen code. It was shit code that barely lasted six months, but it was in the early versions of the apps. Sonny would have rather built the interfaces from scratch; instead he settled for replacing everything Rabbit stole once it couldn't keep up with growth.

A few million people had used it. Between that and Sonny's stance, there would be legal damages. Rabbit would get no help from his side, no chance of pleading dumb and hoping an arbiter would slap him on the wrists. Right now, they had him dead to rights. Rabbit's only move was to drag Together into the mud and make them look as bad as Peared. He hadn't considered that before.

The Valley cares about reputations. Rabbit's was already

shit. He had nothing to lose and everything to gain. This was a new edge.

The first step was to discredit Frank Meyers. Thanks to his divorce, Rabbit had learned a thing or two about restraining orders. He didn't have enough on Frank to file yet, but a pattern was building. He just needed to bait Frank into crossing a line, then call Nadia's lawyer up. Rabbit had underestimated Frank, but he now understood just how invested Frank was in their feud. Rabbit was going to rope a dope him.

Frank Meyers was about to become a big liability for Together and Thorn.

Lawsuits were next up. He didn't have as strong a case as Together. Code has all sorts of legal protections, while business models have none. He could thank the movie studios for that nonsense. Still, Together had copied him closely enough that he could counter file. He'd never win the case, but it wouldn't get tossed out. All he needed was get to discovery and start digging into their files. There'd be something in there he could use.

As for Peared, Rabbit came from the school of Lomansey: "Never write if you can speak; never speak if you can nod; never nod if you can wink." He answered to himself and kept documentation to a bare minimum. Another edge for him.

The real play was to get to Thorn Capital. The firm liked to pretend it was above the fray, but they got down in it just like everyone else. They were the ones that put Frank Meyers after Rabbit. They were the ones that created the Teleportation Industry Alliance and left Peared out. They were the ones that were buying his supplier and shutting down the division that serviced Peared. There was a pattern there. A big nasty institution was trying to put the little guy out of business. Even worse, it wasn't above using physical harm to do so. They wouldn't like that story seeing the light of day. Not one bit. His final edge.

In the grand scheme of things, Together was nothing to Thorn and their reputation was everything. He could make this work. He just needed to set the right trap for Frank.

He felt the wire steady underneath him. Fuck those fucks. It was time to move forward again.

58. ANOTHER CLOSES

They were halfway through coffee in the lobby lounge at the Beverly Hilton. Rabbit had not been in there since they closed Trader Vic's. The place still looked good, but of course it would. He stared across the small table at Terry Walker and studied the man. He hadn't expected so much small talk. Terry was the all business sort. Fifteen minutes in, Rabbit realized he was a curiosity to Terry. His reputation preceded him.

Rabbit decided he'd had enough of being examined. He turned the conversation to the matter at hand.

"You didn't need to do this in person," Rabbit said. "A phone call would have been enough."

"I know, but I was in town and it felt like the right thing to do. I prefer to deliver important news in person. Some people appreciate it."

"It's a nice gesture, but I suspect the news is the news no matter the setting or delivery."

"I suppose," Terry said. A waiter topped their cups up. "Have you spoken with Kendra lately?"

"Not since she was forced out. I should check in on her. She seemed preoccupied just before her 'resignation.' We'd drifted some once Peared assumed a regular operational pattern."

"But she did give you an inkling of what was coming." Terry reached into his jacket pocket, took out his own brand of sweetener, and poured it into his coffee.

"She sure did. I can quote the section of the contract you are about to invoke. Verbatim."

"The part about the six-month wind down period? Well, you know how the mechanics work then." Terry lifted his spoon out of his cup and waved it towards Rabbit. "Here's the verbal notice. Rabbit Wilson, NAM is ending our relationship with Peared. We'll assist you for a period of six months starting today. You'll have our written notice this afternoon."

"There's that news. The coffee here is a lot better than our office, so I suppose there's that. You are shelving Paolo's team?" Rabbit asked.

"We have to. Too many dark arts in there. No other way to sell NAM."

"There's always another way, you know that Terry. Everyone does. My experience is that there's usually only one way to maximize the sale price. Let me guess, this is it."

"That's not something I can discuss with you."

"Nor can you tell me who you are selling it to?" Rabbit leaned in, his voice dropping to a whisper. "You can't tell me that it's Automata?"

Terry put his coffee mug down and looked across at Rabbit. He blinked a couple times, then picked his mug up. It was a tell for sure. Rabbit could read that clear as day.

"No, I can't discuss which parties are involved in the process."

"Of course. I understand." Rabbit leaned back and pushed his chair up onto the back legs. "Tell me this Terry, since we have the time, what would you do in my shoes?"

"I'd sell. Get out while you still can." Terry picked the spoon back up, he looked at it for a moment, then poked it in the air towards Rabbit. "This game is all inside baseball now, and you are an outsider."

"Who says I want to sell?"

"It's not a matter of wanting. It's a matter of getting what you can while there's still something left." The spoon back into the cup, stirring the bottom.

"What're my alternatives?"

"Wither and die. I heard most of your company is following Sonny and moving to Pasadena without you. Now you are losing your back office at NAM. Em and Kendra are gone. Retaining Paolo is very important for us. His group might be done, but we still want him. Don't count on keeping him. That would be a miscalculation. Tell me, when was the last time you hired someone? I'm trying to see a play here Rabbit, but you are suffering from some serious brain drain."

"Yeah, I'm short. Very short." Rabbit's hands rapped the table. "It's been a rather rapid exodus. Could be a miserable coincidence, or someone could be pulling the strings on this. Thorn perhaps."

"Don't flatter yourself, Rabbit. You barely register up there."

"That's not the way I see things. When Automata overpays for NAM, I'll know I don't need glasses. You are carrying water for that asshole and he is paying a premium for it. Look, I appreciate you doing this in person, but give me something I can actually work with Terry. It was a thirty-minute drive for Christ sakes."

"What do you mean?"

"You are shutting my back office down. I get it, your fund's performance comes first, but you just shot my business in the heart. Give me a band-aid at least."

"Look Rabbit, it's nothing personal. You want a band-aid? There is a Dutch company called Garmont that can replace us. They are pricks to do business with, but once you buy their gear, they'll give you top notch support and installation. Get them plugged in early while we are still in a wind down. It will

197

learn how NAM is running Peared and pick up 95% of it. Setup shop offshore. Somewhere cheap. Garmont has a professional services division. Hire them for a year to train your new people and it will be like you never missed a beat."

"Garmont huh? They've been pestering me for a meeting for months."

"Look into them, Rabbit. Like I said, they are pricks to negotiate with, but you seem like the sort that can manage that. If you want to go it alone, that's your best bet for remaining independent."

Rabbit finished his coffee. "Thanks Terry. I appreciate that. I'm not done yet. You'll see."

"Rabbit, if you want to take the more sensible road, call me up. I know a few people that would buy you."

"Thorn had a chance to be sensible. I'm afraid we're all well past that now."

59. STATELESS

Paolo closed the door and collapsed on his office couch. It was hot out and smog had settled over the Valley. He wished he was at Zion, his foot jammed against rock, his eyes scanning for the next hold. Instead, he had just wrapped an all-hands meeting with his team. He listened with the rest of the group as Terry Walker broke the news. Automata had bought NAM for an impressive $1.3 billion in stock. As part of the transaction, all non-core businesses would be wound down.

The news was hard to take. Terry had already notified Peared they were done with them. He hadn't told the team anything about their future. Maybe there'd be opportunities here. Maybe there wouldn't be.

Kendra always treated Paolo like talent first and a manager second. He returned results, he didn't set HR policy. If she was doing this, they'd have information packets with severance details, job placement resources, and transition milestones in it. Instead he had Terry who wanted nothing to do with this stepchild account.

"You have the money and the means. Figure it out. The only thing I care about is that the doors shut on July 14th," he had told Paolo.

Meanwhile, he was pressing Paolo hard to join Automata. Paolo politely told him to go fuck himself. The narrowness of Terry offered no appeal. He knew Paolo produced and that was all he cared about. He didn't care about the mess Paolo had to clean up first. He didn't care about the personal promises Paolo had made, promises that were now empty. Paolo resolved to strip this place to the bone, load the employee bonus pool up, and give his people the largest walking package he could muster up. His share included.

Paolo didn't need that money anymore. He had $3 million waiting for him in Panama. That was the silver lining. Money changed his feelings about hanging around for his green card. Without a need to earn in USD, he was starting to see the world with new eyes. He had a lot more options whether he wanted to stay here or go abroad.

Earlier in the week, Rabbit had come calling looking for him to join Peared. He turned him down, too. Kendra had been right. Without those centaur jobs, he'd be facing much harder choices. Now, he was looking at the situation on his terms. Whatever was next for Paolo, was what Paolo wanted. No one else. All his life he had served. Family, school, work. In six months, he'd have no masters and no obligations. If he was smart and took a couple more jobs, he'd have $4, maybe $5 million waiting for him. At that point he could do whatever he wanted. He could finally become his own man.

Maybe Monica would be by his side, maybe not. He hoped so, but he'd been alone long enough to know it wasn't a fatal condition.

60. TIJUANA DUTCH

In the end, it was the obvious move. Rabbit only regretted not making it sooner. After Sonny walked, the tech team started to bleed out. A couple staffers a week turned in their notice and joined him in Pasadena. Word was getting around town that something was rotten inside Rabbit's company. Recruiting was tough. His candidate flow was full of hacks. Paper tigers whose resumes hadn't done anything interesting in years and expected A-level compensation. He knew these fools. They passed themselves off as polished, accomplished, capable, but all they did was blend in with the carpet. Only the bloated or the desperate hired retreads like them.

He looked at his list of assets. He had the Sams who stayed on. He thought they had a beef with Automata, but who could tell with them. He had Omar, who was hungry as always. He had Garmont who they signed with last week. Everyone else was a liability. Sure, there was some steady workers left, but they were unspectacular and completely replaceable. Especially when he could do it at half the cost.

Rabbit was leading Peared into the desert, or at least close enough for his liking. He brought Omar out of the call center, installed him as general manager, and they began the process of turning that building into their new HQ. He wanted to be completely out of LA by May. Anyone who lasted that long would get two week's severance and could then file for unemployment.

Peared's performance would suffer during this transition,

but a fresh start was needed. Tijuana was their future.

Twelve years earlier, Rabbit had burnt out before he realized the sort of people he worked best with. After that Ka$ia kept him on a tight leash, his behavior closely watched. Now, two and a half years into Peared, he realized that people were nothing but a set of hands for him. He could think for the entire company, he could see for the entire company, he just needed mercenaries who would march and fight when told. California was soft. It was full of group think, double talk, and glad handers. When things were good, everyone wanted to contribute, but once it got tough, they cleared out quick. NAM's sale was a blessing. It opened his eyes and forced him to make radical choices. Once he was away from LA, its distractions and petulant demands, he could focus entirely on the battle at hand.

61. PILLOW TALK

After three days of meetings in Tijuana, it took Paolo two hours to cross the border and another three and a half to get to Santa Monica. She had been waiting for him at the Casa Del Mar, in a corner suite overlooking the beach. She jumped him the moment he walked in the door, not bothering with the drapes or doors. Had it been any later in the season, they would have drawn attention. Instead, an indifferent ocean observed without comment.

They lay naked under the white down comforter, two bodies entwined as one. Pillow talk inevitably turned to business; this time it was Paolo who broached the subject.

"We've got a three-week window and then it's over," he said.

"So soon?"

"Rabbit is possessed. The man is driving everyone as hard as they'll work. He's got Garmont doing OT and weekends. They'll be putting their instrumentation into the service in three weeks. After that, they can monitor everything. If I'm Rabbit, my first priority is making sure that God Mode is wired for sound. There's no one left that he trusts."

"He's paranoid, but he's not technically wrong. He just can't see the forest for the trees. Not my problem, and soon enough, it won't be yours. So, Paolo are you up for one last job?"

"Depends."

She turned over in the bed and faced him. "On?"

"The money, the location, the type of work. Needs to be a Goldilocks situation. Give me something just right and I'll do it. Did you and Malcolm talk about Kendra?"

"We did."

"And?"

"Well, we didn't know how things were going to go, so we talked about two options. If this was an ongoing thing, we'd push her aside gently. If we were only doing one or two jobs, we felt we'd keep her in. Just so she doesn't leave with any hard feelings. No reason to get greedy and screw it all up."

"I'm fine with that."

"Paolo?" Monica sat up in the bed.

"Yes."

"How come you've never asked about you and me?"

Paolo looked up at her. "You mean when this whole thing is over?"

"Yes."

"Because I don't want you to lie to me."

"Who says I'll lie to you?"

"If you say nothing, there's zero chance you do. If you say something, it's fifty-fifty."

"That's cruel, Paolo."

"Monica, I'll be here after. All you need to do is the same."

She pulled the covers off and got out of the bed. He watched her walk away. A few seconds later the shower started. He could have, should have handled that better, but now the moment had passed. He'd made his point but hurt her in the process. Maybe she really did care. He'd find out soon enough. In three weeks, he'd be just Paolo. Not an asset, not a pawn, just a man who cared deeply for her. She'd either come back for him or she wouldn't.

If she had lied now, it'd be that much harder when she didn't.

62. TIRED BUT TRUE

It was cheap, it was a cliché, but it would work. Rabbit remembered when his marriage was breaking up. He teetered on the edge of control, a cauldron of anger, everything a recrimination. He'd never run into Diana's lover during that shitshow, but if he had, he'd have broken his jaw.

Frank was a cheater. Maybe he'd cleaned his act up since they worked together, but Rabbit doubted it. Once a poon hound, always a poon hound.

He'd gone north alone. His wife Alice, and two kids stayed behind in Beverly Hills. "Smallest house on the block," he'd always say, "but we're there for the schools". He likely flew up on Mondays and came down on Thursdays. That left three long lonely nights. Now that he'd nailed Rabbit, Frank probably didn't have anything to occupy his time. A man like that is going to get fidgety.

Frank liked doing speaking engagements. Industry shit, some mentoring, lessons from a life in technology. His LinkedIn showed three coming up. Two in the Bay Area. After a speech he liked to hit the lobby bar and hold court for a bit. Friends would come by and tell him what a good job he'd done. Rabbit had caught his act more than once, and it was always the same. That would be the time to hit him. Get some cute little thing. Smart looking, but sexy. The type Hollywood cast as the nerd. She'd have to be bright enough to talk the talk, but enough of a pro to trap him on tape.

After that, it was as simple as sending an anonymous attachment to Alice. She was not going to take that quietly. Frank would be out on the street, and he'd know just who set him up. All Rabbit needed to do after that was be in the right place at the wrong time. Somewhere public, somewhere Frank would lose it on him. Oh, he could see it now. An unhinged rant ending in a punch. Rabbit would go down like a pussy. He'd crumble in a heap whether Frank really connected or not.

Someone would tape that too. He'd get a restraining order, then file a second lawsuit. This one accusing Thorn Capital of a pattern of harassment. They set this whole thing in motion and look where it led. Rabbit fled to Mexico just to be able to work freely; he comes back for a weekend and then this happens?

Not a good look. Not a good look at all.

63. NETWORK CONTROL

The just right job fell into Paolo's lap. He thanked Monica and watched as she walked over to the edge of the deck. The back of her feet popped out of her heels; she stretched her legs and pulled herself higher to look down into the canyon below. Still no sign of Kendra and Malcolm. She sighed and wandered off, tired of being up in the hills, ready to get moving on their next assignment. Time was short, and she valued hers like no one else.

Paolo thumbed through the materials—Imran Malik's Wikipedia entry, news articles from Dawn and Geo, a summary of the political situation in Karachi. All useful background, but the *why* did not really matter. He was searching for the specs, the requirements that would dictate the work.

Paolo was a *How* man, not a *Why* man.

He found them held together in a clip, one of those large black and silver ones common on legal files. Flipping through, he saw page after page of Peared profiles. Glad that the bulk of the file was data and not asks, he went back to the beginning and started to read.

Ten minutes later, a shadow fell over him. Monica was back from wherever. He knew she was exasperated by the way she clicked her tongue against the roof of her mouth. Malcolm and Kendra were clearly not here.

"Yes?" Paolo asked.

"We are going on thirty minutes now."

"Is that a problem for you?"

"If he was *working* late that'd be one thing, but he's *fucking her* late."

"How do you know?"

"He called. He said he'd be here in twenty. They are still at her hotel. Forty minutes in this traffic. I could hear the shower running."

"Wasn't that just us a few days ago?"

"Yes, but no one was waiting on me."

He watched her storm off. His mind returned to the task at hand. It didn't matter to him whether they were on time or not. Even if they were here, he'd need time to run through the job. He had to think of edge cases and failure points. Actions make ripples in the pond. Those ripples collide. Sometimes they quietly cancel each other, other times they push together and become a larger force which then needs to be accounted for.

Their client wanted Paolo to act as a controller of the Peared network so that Imran Malik, the People's Lion, could march from his party's storefront headquarters in Clifton to a rally in the Defense neighborhood. Malik was a rising star who lacked the muscle and infrastructure of the entrenched PQP party. Overseas organizers wanted to pair with Hands on the ground to bolster their confidence, give them the courage to march, and get Malik to his destination. Paolo couldn't tell if that task mattered more than the inverse, which was keeping PQP operatives from forming Pairs.

Either way, it was a simple, but laborious, job. Karachi was a big market for them. There'd be thousands of users online. He had to create a one-mile radius around Malik while also connecting the attached list of Eyes and preventing others from pairing. He wouldn't need to talk to any of them. He didn't need to dictate any actions. He just needed to grant their client exclusive control of the network near Malik.

It could be done. The tricky part was in the reporting. If he was blocking Eyes, they could file error reporting. A couple thousand of those concentrated in one locality would trigger alerts. If something happened that day, there would be evidence that someone was tampering with the system. The alerts wouldn't point to anything further, but they would stand as a starting clue.

The risk was acceptable to Paolo. He'd be gone after this. Besides it was Karachi. The Pakistani government routinely shut the entire internet off and had some serious injection capabilities. Everyone would view this as an internal matter and leave it at that.

Happy with the solution, he was ready for the briefing. Malcolm and Kendra still hadn't showed.

It was Paolo's turn to be annoyed.

64. DECIPHER

They worked out of the canyon house in Malibu. Four stations were set, but only Paolo and Monica were present. Paolo didn't know if the two of them could handle it, but he liked the cadence of their prior job. Downtown LA had gone crisply; there was an easy interplay back and forth. No questioning, just a commitment to the task at hand, and a willingness to get it done. Still, this was a lot more people and a completely different protocol. He kept Malcolm and Kendra on standby with orders to be at the ready.

Karachi was like nowhere he'd ever worked before. He had spent the last couple days peering into it from God Mode. A ghost in the shell, hitching rides behind unsuspecting Eyes. It was big like Los Angeles, busy like Hong Kong, and armed like Johannesburg. It was raw, on edge, but quite comfortably bursting at the seams. No one could thrive here without giving way to the unceasing current that drove the city.

It was a place that recognized higher power.

Paolo was told to not connect to anyone too close to the Rangers, the military presence in the city. Like everywhere in Pakistan, the army had the ultimate say in what went on. They were posted around the city, never moving unless necessary, but visible and undisputed. They would not act unless the city was about to spin out of control, and Karachi had a very liberal definition of control.

Malik's office was upstairs in a shopping arcade off Khayaban-e-Iqbal road. They were marching two and a half miles south to Zamzama Park where ten thousand would meet them. Hundreds had gathered outside, filling the parking lot, squeezed between cars. A brightly decorated bus would lead the march, and another would bring up the rear. Drumwallas pounded out a driving rhythm, then the candidate descended into the lobby, and the crowd erupted. They were a confident group, Paolo didn't see why outsiders were needed, but he didn't know the place, the people, or the politics.

He simply knew his protocol.

Paolo stopped watching the scene and went to work. Malik's body man was wearing a pair of AR glasses. He would not leave his boss's side and would be the center of the moving perimeter. Paolo flagged him in God Mode and placed a one-mile connection quarantine zone around him. That safety feature meant no Eyes could connect with anyone in the zone unless they were whitelisted. It also meant that any pair which wandered into the zone would have their connection dropped.

He looked over at Monica and nodded. Each had a stack of papers from the dossier in front of them. They began pulling up Peared usernames, whitelisting one after another and allowing them to connect in the zone. These were their clients, the outside supporters who had bought network exclusivity from Malcolm. He looked at the map. Forty red dots indicated their people. Two hundred yellow dots indicated available Hands. Ten dimmed out dots indicated blocked Eyes.

They began pulling profiles and connecting Pairs together. He listened in to them.

"This man is our brother," they shouted. "Our time is here."

The front bus started forward and the people spilled out of the parking lot into the main thoroughfare. His pairs had switched to Urdu and he lost the conversation except for occasional snippets of "bhai" or brother, the only word Paolo knew. For the rest of the march, the job was to keep rotating their Eyes through the pool of Hands.

Paolo managed the connections, while Monica kept watch through the feeds of multiple Hands. As the parade made its way across town, Pairs would break away from the marchers and pull people into the crowd. Malik's marchers swelled, doubling, then tripling in size. No one stood in their way, no one opposed them. Paolo kept his eyes on the map in God Mode. If the PQP tried to get into the network, the number of dimmed-out dots would increase. The dots grew, but only in proportion to the size of the overall crowd.

The march turned the corner, and there was the reason they'd been hired. The street was blocked with truck containers, arranged across the length of the road, making it impassable. The marchers, now over a thousand strong, slowed down, then came to a stop. Eyes sprang into action, exhorting the crowd. Pushing glamour effects and Malik's campaign song into their Hands' ears.

"There's another way."

"We will be heard. We will be seen. We will continue."

"We cannot stop. The people await us in the park."

The Eyes were now rapidly connecting, then dropping, working their way through the crowd. They were like border collies directing the crowd down a side road in an attempt to cut parallel to Zamzama Blvd. Slowly the people got in gear, squeezing down the narrower street. Paolo watched Malik being pressed to the front. Pairs concentrated on the sides and rear, herding people in.

"I don't like this, Paolo. Too many people, too small a space," Monica said.

"The body man just turned, he's moving away from the crowd."

"Find someone on the other side. Connect into them. See what these people are walking into."

Paolo didn't want to risk exposing himself. He lifted the

quarantine and waited for someone—anyone nearby—to pair up so he could watch through their connection.

"Paolo, all our Eyes just went offline."

"I dropped the quarantine. Do you think it spooked them?"

"How would I know?"

"I'm connecting in now."

They looked up at the monitor. The crowd, with Imran Malik at the front, pushed their way down the side street. Their early singing had given way to defiance. They marched forward, chanting, shaking their fists. Banners spanning the length of the narrow block waved and rocked with pictures of Malik. Then the screen went white. All connections dropped from the map.

"Please tell me the government cut internet," Paolo muttered and stared helplessly.

Twenty minutes later, their worst fears were confirmed. A bomb planted behind a wall in the street had exploded, killing Malik, and dozens more. It had been a hit job. The People's Lion would roar no more.

Monica sat stoically, staring out into space, glassy-eyed.

"Did you know about this?" Paolo asked.

"How dare you."

"Did you know about this?"

"No."

"Call Malcolm. Get him up here."

"You do it, you shit."

"I don't have his number."

She threw her phone at him and walked out to the deck. His unsteady hands dialed Malcolm as hers tried to light a cigarette.

It had all gone wrong.

65. LINES

Saturday morning at the Grove. A matinee movie, a sesame bagel, and a large coffee. It was one of Rabbit's favorite things to do in this town. He'd been coming once a month since he first arrived decades ago. While so much had come and gone, this little tradition was still there for him.

He hadn't made up his mind yet, either *Gaston! A Hunter's Tale* or *Son of Shrek*, but it didn't really matter. If he didn't like one, he'd just walk into the other. That was the nice part about this time of day. Things were quiet. You could park on the second floor of the garage and you didn't need to fight through a million idiots. No strollers, no shopping bags, no yappy little dogs.

Beating the inconveniences kept him in love with Los Angeles.

The movie started ten minutes ago, which meant it would be another fifteen before they wrapped the commercials and trailers. Rabbit sat on a bench eating his bagel. Better to get that done first. He'd ruined several shirts eating runny cream cheese in darkened theaters.

He was about to take a bite when he felt a rap on the back of his head. Not a tap, not a slap, but a swift enough whack that it got his attention real fast. He looked up and saw Frank standing there red-faced, veins throbbing, finger poking him in the chest hard.

This fucking guy. He wasn't supposed to be here now. Who

gets thrown out of the house and then comes to the mall first thing on a Saturday?

"Whoa back off," Rabbit said.

"I know what you fucking did, Rabbit."

There it was, another finger in his chest. Rabbit jerked and spit out his coffee, splattering it on Frank's khaki pants.

"Back off Frank. I'm trying to eat here."

"I know it was fucking you."

"Me what?"

"You sent that video to Alice."

"What video?"

"The video."

"Again, what video?"

"The one of me cheating on her."

"Ok. Here we go again. You blame me for something you did."

"I know it was fucking you."

"No, it was you fucking someone Frank. Don't look at me. I'm down in Mexico because your masters took my people. Not my problem that you hopped on the first piece that batted her eyes at you. What happened, you didn't pay her afterwards?"

And there was the finger in his chest again. This time Rabbit squeezed his coffee so the lid popped off and spilled all over Frank's leg. Frank jumped back, and Rabbit started to stand.

"I asked you to stop touching me."

Before Rabbit could straighten out, he felt the big right hook come crashing down on the side of his head. He heard a sickly noise, finger bones breaking as they slammed into skull. He felt his left ear catch on fire, prickling with a million tingling embers, then a brief second of stillness before the ringing started. Rabbit fell to the ground. A moment later the broadside of a shoe caught his ribs. That wasn't too bad, Rabbit thought.

Frank changed his stance and connected, tip wedging between bones, driving inside his chest cavity.

Fuck. That hurt. It hurt badly.

It was the first of many.

Rabbit started to hyperventilate. Wheezing and gasping as kick after kick connected against the side of his chest. This wasn't the beating he'd imagined taking.

It stopped after a minute. He looked up through blurred eyes as strangers pulled Frank back. He tried to stand, get the last word in, but pain stabbed him. He coughed out a sickly red tinged mucus, then curled into the fetal position. He didn't think Frank had that much rage in him.

Moments went by. Security pulled Frank away. Rabbit began to laugh wickedly. His broken ribs stung like motherfuckers, but he couldn't stop himself. So many people, so many fucking cameras here, such a one-sided fight. This was the end of Frank. When this was all said and done, Rabbit would own him. He was finished.

Time to move up the tree and knock those fucks at Thorn off their perch.

First, he needed an ambulance.

66. HOME AWAY

Paolo wanted to go home, but where was that? Santiago, which he left at seventeen. Los Gatos to his company housing?

Thirty-two years old and Paolo had not made a place for himself. Now he had nothing to return to. He'd made it as far as LAX and then stopped, checking into the Hyatt Regency on Century. Loyalty rewards got him upgraded into a suite. It was a nice for what it was. They'd put money into the soundproofing. Two flat screens and a partition between the bedroom and the living room.

He turned on the TV and went looking for BBC News. No American network would carry the explosion. This country was done being concerned about others. It could barely muster up interest in the latest school shooting.

Paolo finally cared and what had it taken? He helped kill seventy-eight people today. The worst part, no one would know what a monster he was. No one would look him in the eyes and call him to account. He was just another faceless man coasting through the air space of society. He had filled his life with puzzles and problems, immune to their reality. The last seven years were an abstraction. The only real thing he ever did was climb, and what was that? A man alone on a rock, inching upwards simply because it's there.

He needed Monica. He needed to blackout and take his punishment.

Paolo didn't believe Malcolm and Kendra. They claimed to

have been played. Said they were doing this for friends who wanted to make a difference. Malcolm even showed him the wires. It was a tiny amount compared to their other jobs. The money had all been earmarked for Paolo. They were working pro bono.

It sounded too convenient. Like another kind of work.

His phone was off. He hadn't been online since he called a Lyft from the bottom of the canyon. He wanted to talk to someone, but who? He had kept such a narrow life. Kendra was his confessor and now he didn't trust her. Monica was hurt badly today, but she was complicit to a point. He couldn't tell how deep she went.

He didn't trust the internet. He couldn't post anonymously somewhere. Look what he did to Peared. Everything was rotten, it was all a big fix.

He saw three choices. Ball it all up deep inside and make tomorrow the first new day of his life, call the FBI and confess, or head back to the people who knew how to fix him, even if it was the same people that had broken him. Whatever he did, he needed to stay offline until the shock passed.

Actually, there was one more idea. He could go to Rabbit. It was his company, his platform that was at risk. Rabbit hadn't a clue what they were using Peared for. He was too busy fighting the Valley to see what was happening under his nose. Didn't he have a right to know? But what did Paolo hope to get from that? He could entrap the others, and then flip them to law enforcement. That seemed far-fetched. More likely, Rabbit would just patch God Mode ahead of schedule.

Rabbit had offered to help him; he said he understood bad shit. He had offered Paolo a job. Was that what Paolo was looking for? A replacement for Kendra? Someone to clean up his mess? He decided to call Em. She had a handle on Rabbit's personality. She could advise him. He picked up the room phone and dialed.

"Em here."

"Hey Em, long time no talk. It's Paolo. Do you have a couple minutes?"

"I can give you five tops, then I need to get back on set. What's up?"

"I'm in a situation. I need some advice."

"Okay. Not sure why are you asking me, but what can I do?"

"You understand Rabbit. Not a lot of people do."

"Kendra does. If you aren't asking her, then it's because she's involved."

"Something like that."

"And if Kendra is involved, so is money."

"Yes."

"Paolo, when you answer this question, just a simple one-word answer will do. I don't want any details at all. This money, when Rabbit finds out about it, will he feel entitled to none, some, or all of it?"

"Some at least, maybe all."

"Don't tell me anything else. Here's the deal Paolo. If you cheated him or somehow shorted him, he's not capable of forgiving you. I don't care what he told you in the past, if you hurt him then he'll come for you. I have real regrets about leaving Peared. That was a challenge worthy of me, but Rabbit is Rabbit. Don't ask him for something he can't do."

" Even if I tried to make it right?"

"No. Not now. He needs to grow up first. All of you do. Whatever you are doing, knock it off and try to act like an adult."

"I understand. Thanks, Em."

"Good luck with your problem Paolo."

Paolo hung the phone up. He was back to his original choices and didn't know how to feel about them. He went to his bag and looked for the Ambien he kept on hand. If anything, tomorrow was another day. He might have a better idea then.

67. SUNSEEKER

He woke up in the mid-morning haze. The fog was burning off, but the pain was still there. Paolo reconsidered his options, then he walked to Carl's Jr. hoping that a new one would emerge. Instead, the choices narrowed. Paolo was in a closed loop. Walking away now would make him an unhandled error condition, and he didn't want to be a trouble ticket.

It would result in the termination of his process.

Going to the FBI was also off the table. He wasn't a citizen. He had no idea what they would do to him, but whether he stayed in the US or was handed over to the ISI, it would be beyond horrible.

No. His only choice was burying it and if he couldn't, then he'd have to find another way to make amends.

He picked at his hash rounds, popping them into his mouth and rubbing the oil between his fingertips. Food felt good, even if it was the cheapest of carbs. He needed to get his energy back for tonight. The proper way out was to complete the program. Malcolm needed to see his agents within their operating parameters, so he could shut everything down. Paolo needed to turn himself over, release control, and stand there devoid of will. Malcolm would probe and push him. Paolo would show that he would not crack, then Malcolm would punish him, so that Paolo could start over.

The following morning, he'd find out what Monica really felt. If she came to him, then rebuilding would be that much easier. If she turned on him, then it was the hardest lesson he'd ever learn. Either way, it was time he started really living. Paolo was too capable an operator to live in abstractions. Abstracted, his actions got people hurt.

No, they killed people. A lot of them.

And now he must atone for that. He turned his iPhone on. Monica picked up on the first ring.

"Paolo. Where are you?"

"Close. I'm still in LA. I want to come back. I need to purge. We need to finish this. Am I safe?"

"Of course, you are. We are all fucked up Paolo. You're not alone on this one."

Her voice was cracked, haggard, he heard her sniffling.

"How long have you been crying?"

"All night, asshole. I thought you left me."

Pure emotion. Despite himself, he smiled because she cared.

"I'm sorry, Monica. I just lost my shit."

"You said you'd be here."

"Should I come now?"

"No. Now that I've heard from you, I need to sleep. It will be a long night. Meet us at the Sunseeker at eight."

He put his phone down and picked up his breakfast burrito. See, it wasn't that hard. Just bite and chew. Once you are done, throw your wrappers away and walk on out the door. Something else will be waiting for you. Keep on moving, keep something else always in sight.

Soon enough, this will all be done, and she'll be there.

68. WHITE BORDEAUX

Paolo arrived at eight. He was wearing the same outfit from Mastro's. White linen pants, black t-shirt, boat shoes. His commitment to burying Karachi had built throughout the day, and he was confident that nothing lurked beneath that thought. He would stand up just fine.

Kendra stood on the deck waiting for him. She was in white. Her eyes a bit glassy, he could tell she had been in the wine. He didn't blame her. He had a few himself before coming over. They hugged. He felt her warmth against his chest, pulling him in. Malcolm walked up behind her, his big paw reaching over Kendra and landing on Paolo's shoulder in sympathy. Paolo looked him in the eye, they nodded at each other. It was enough.

Monica emerged from the cabin, the final member of their party. She was in the coral dress he loved so much. She walked behind Paolo and pressed herself against his back, her hands wrapping under his arms, her face nestled between his shoulder blades. The four of them held tight, the tender moment necessary to grant permission for what was to come. They all needed forgiving.

The foursome rocked with the gentle motion of the boat. Tears streamed down from Kendra, Monica. Paolo felt both sides of his shirt go damp. His eyes went blurry, but he couldn't cry.

Finally, Monica pulled away.

"White Bordeaux?" she asked Paolo.

"Yes, please."

She sat next to him, they toasted and drank. Halfway through he began to feel fuzzy. He thought he saw Kendra reaching in, taking their glasses. Then it went black.

69. CABERNET SAUVIGNON

"One last time?" Malcolm asked, his head cocked in the direction of Paolo and Monica.

"I can't," Kendra replied.

Malcolm started up the big boat. He pulled her away from the slip and out of the marina. The yacht passed the breakwater, out into the ocean.

"Why her?" Kendra finally asked.

"Because she fell for him."

A mile out, he dropped anchor. Kendra tidied up as Malcolm carried Paolo then Monica below deck to the stateroom. He came back up and joined Kendra on the deck. They drank a bottle of cab in silence. The boat looked back at LA, the planes taking off, the lights snaking up the hills, the huge hulking basin. The last glass finished, a signal for action. She looked at Malcolm.

"It's time," she said.

"I'll do it," he said, standing up.

"If you don't mind."

Malcolm went below deck. He took the small leather dap kit from the cabinet above the fridge. Gloves went on. Needles came out. The first plunged into Monica, the next into Paolo. Eyes fluttered, lips trembled, he watched their chests rise and fall, rise and fall, then stop moving. He staged the scene and then went above board.

He flipped a switch and the anchor came up. The boat began back towards the marina.

"Tell me the story," Malcolm said quietly.

"We had drinks, we went for a cruise. They couldn't keep their hands off each other. We felt like a third wheel, so we decided to cut things short and let them have the boat for the night. We docked, then left the marina at ten and went back to your place. Neither of us had any idea they were into that sort of thing. We thought they wanted to have sex, not shoot up. I'm shocked."

70. ONE YEAR LATER

Rabbit started Peared to show LA they made a mistake. They had cut the wrong guy out sooner than he deserved. So, he waited and watched. He stayed in the place he loved, and he took what they gave him.

That all changed when his father passed. He finally had the money to create the product that kept him up at night. The special idea, the one that someone would back despite Rabbit's past sins. Only, he had been too paranoid to share it, so kept it to himself until he had the means to make it on his terms.

It was paranoia well served.

Peared was the right idea at the right time. It had been squirreled away in Rabbit's brain, waiting until the moment when the world was ready to walk with the internet in their eyes. Everything came together perfectly, and Peared became a monster. The monster had served him well, that is until the Valley saw what he had done.

They wanted his creation and wouldn't leave him alone.

Rabbit's father taught him there was no satisfaction in sharing, only people who wanted to take your best from you. He didn't want to be the godfather of an idea. He wanted to be the sole proprietor. Teleportation belonged to him.

Only when an idea this big comes along, the Valley doesn't see an owner. It sees a new cash cow, and everyone tries to milk it. Except this time, the inventor didn't fit the neat little narrative of the hero founder. Rabbit was crass, he had an ugly past, and he didn't belong on magazine covers. When the Valley came calling, looking to buy, he turned down generational wealth.

They were trying to buy him off.

His idea was amazing, but he wasn't good enough for it. Rabbit couldn't stomach that, so a fight for LA became a fight for California.

Who was Peter Thorn? Why did he feel entitled to what Rabbit willed into the world? That's where Rabbit stopped and asked, just exactly what did he want.

Rabbit was a man who wanted to dominate. He wanted his fiefdom and the freedom to rule it.

So, it got ugly.

No one who launched Peared worked there anymore. Frank Meyers was in jail. Paolo dead. Kendra selling condos. The SEC was investigating Automata. Rabbit was on his third lawsuit against Thorn Capital.

Now he was in Mexico. He was protected. Rabbit had given the country a new border industry to go with the maquiladoras and call centers. He had brought tech to a place where no one gave a fuck about Peter Thorn. Rabbit had serious weight, and a lot of money. He could stay here and do this forever.

People had said Rabbit was paranoid, but he had been right all along. They had all been after his special idea. Now they couldn't touch him.

It had given him such sweet satisfaction to watch Rizon go up in flames.

One more thing Rabbit saw from miles away.

All that stood between Rabbit and his goal was Thorn and Together. Together was ground down. Omar had done his job. It had barely two million active users, the churn rate was abysmal, and the Sams estimated customer acquisition was now around $180. That company was going broke.

He hit play on the video for the fifth time this morning. Peter Thorn was on a stage in New Zealand announcing a $250 million-dollar investment in Together. This time he noticed that Aussie giant in the background, DuBour. How had Rabbit missed him before? He'd been in the shadows this entire time. Kendra, Paolo, and NAM all wiped off the map, and this fucker was there. Now he's on stage as Thorn triples down on his bad bet? Fuck. He had missed something, but now he knew DuBour was an enemy.

Rabbit had miscalculated. He thought Thorn was one and done, that he wouldn't throw good money after bad. Rabbit had been thinking too small. All this fighting had been personal. He wondered what else he'd missed. He never considered the broader implications of his creation. Now he realized just how valuable Peared was. Rabbit was no longer fighting against California. He wasn't just fighting against Thorn. He was fighting for his place in history.

Thorn was throwing good money after bad because he couldn't afford to lose something as important as teleportation.

With Peared, Rabbit had the chance to be a conqueror on an unparalleled level. Fuck Alexander, fuck Khan, fuck Thorn. Rabbit's product was in the eyes of 400 million people, telling them what to do, where to go, how to act. That was true power.

Now that he understood, he would never give it up. He leaned back in his chair and thought about how right that was.

"This is the last network, and it's mine."

What he didn't think about was the statistical improbability of it all. Rabbit had defied the odds. He'd never given a thought to the hands of fate. Was Rabbit right because he was smarter than everyone, or had he just won fifty consecutive coin flips?

What about all those people who only got one flip and lost?

He didn't think about those people because they didn't matter.

Only Rabbit mattered.

Fuck everyone else.

Made in the USA
Coppell, TX
15 January 2020